A Dangerous Game . . .

Spencer stared at me, frowning, biting his bottom lip. "I can't believe it, Diane!" he said finally. His voice trembled. He dug in the pocket of his jeans and pulled out a note. "Look at this."

I glanced at it—the same handwriting as on Cassie's note. "Cassie got one, too," I told him. "She and Lenny are already here. Come in."

He followed me to the den. He nodded to Lenny and Cassie.

"Spencer got a note, too," I said. "It looks just like Cassie's."

"I found it stuck under the windshield wiper of my car," Spencer reported.

"What does it say?" Lenny asked.

Spencer looked down at the note and read it aloud: "'Night games can be dangerous. Sometimes people die.'"

Books by R. L. Stine

FEAR STREET
THE NEW GIRL
THE SURPRISE PARTY
THE OVERNIGHT
MISSING
THE WRONG NUMBER
THE SLEEPWALKER
HAUNTED
HALLOWEEN PARTY
THE STEPSISTER
SKI WEEKEND
THE FIRE GAME
LIGHTS OUT
THE SECRET BEDROOM
THE KNIFE
PROM QUEEN
FIRST DATE
THE BEST FRIEND
THE CHEATER
SUNBURN
THE NEW BOY
THE DARE
BAD DREAMS
DOUBLE DATE
THE THRILL CLUB
ONE EVIL SUMMER
THE MIND READER
WRONG NUMBER 2
TRUTH OR DARE
DEAD END
FINAL GRADE
SWITCHED
COLLEGE WEEKEND
THE STEPSISTER 2
WHAT HOLLY HEARD
THE FACE
SECRET ADMIRER
THE PERFECT DATE
THE CONFESSION
THE BOY NEXT DOOR
NIGHT GAMES

FEAR STREET SUPER CHILLERS
PARTY SUMMER
SILENT NIGHT
GOODNIGHT KISS
BROKEN HEARTS
SILENT NIGHT 2
THE DEAD LIFEGUARD
CHEERLEADERS: THE NEW EVIL
BAD MOONLIGHT
THE NEW YEAR'S PARTY
GOODNIGHT KISS 2

THE FEAR STREET SAGA
THE BETRAYAL
THE SECRET
THE BURNING
FEAR STREET SAGA COLLECTOR'S
  EDITION

FEAR STREET CHEERLEADERS
THE FIRST EVIL
THE SECOND EVIL
THE THIRD EVIL

99 FEAR STREET: THE HOUSE OF EVIL
THE FIRST HORROR
THE SECOND HORROR
THE THIRD HORROR

THE CATALUNA CHRONICLES
THE EVIL MOON
THE DARK SECRET
THE DEADLY FIRE

FEAR STREET SAGAS
A NEW FEAR
HOUSE OF WHISPERS
FORBIDDEN SECRETS

FEAR PARK
THE FIRST SCREAM
THE LOUDEST SCREAM
THE LAST SCREAM

Available from ARCHWAY Paperbacks

FEAR STREET®
R·L·STINE

Night Games

A Parachute Press Book

AN ARCHWAY PAPERBACK
Published by POCKET BOOKS
New York   London   Toronto   Sydney   Tokyo   Singapore

AN ARCHWAY PAPERBACK *Original*

 An Archway Paperback published by
POCKET BOOKS, a division of Simon & Schuster Inc.
1230 Avenue of the Americas, New York, NY 10020

ISBN: 0-671-52958-7

First Archway Paperback printing November 1996

10 9 8 7 6 5 4 3 2 1

FEAR STREET is a registered trademark of Parachute Press, Inc.

AN ARCHWAY PAPERBACK and colophon are registered trademarks of Simon & Schuster Inc.

Cover art by Bill Schmidt

Printed in the U.S.A.

IL 7+

Night Games

chapter

1

"Whoooa!" I stopped and grabbed Lenny Boyle's arm. "Check it *out!*"

I had to shield my eyes against the harsh, bright lights. Lenny laughed and pretended to stagger off the sidewalk.

Cassie Wylant and Jordan Townes were half a block back, arguing again. They had been fighting all night, even while they were dancing. Sometimes I wonder why Cassie and Jordan go together. They're always breaking up, then making up, then breaking up again.

"Helllllooo!" I called, trying to get their attention. "Take a break, guys. You've got to see this!"

They stopped and gawked at the amazing sight. Even Cassie had to laugh. It's hard to get Cassie to laugh. She's a great friend, but she really doesn't have much of a sense of humor.

In fact, she's the most serious person in our crowd.

Always study, study, study. It was great seeing her lighten up and dance at Red Heat tonight. Her copper-colored hair was flying. Her hazel eyes reflected the flashing lights.

If only she and Jordan didn't fight all the time.

He's so good looking—and he knows it. And he's always coming on to other girls. I think that's what starts most of their fights. I don't know for sure.

Cassie and I are good friends. But Cassie sort of keeps herself tightly wrapped up. She doesn't reveal what she's really thinking—not even to me.

But now, walking home from the dance club, we were all thinking the same thing: How could Mr. Crowell do this to his front yard?

All four of us stopped and stared at the brightest, ugliest, craziest, *tackiest* display of Christmas lights we'd ever seen! Red and green lights blazed from the roof, around the windows and doors, along the gutters—and in all the trees!

Mr. Crowell had *two* Santas facing each other in identical, glowing sleighs. Reindeer with flashing red noses, elves, gremlins, Santa's helpers, bright purple mice, bright white snowmen, neon animals I didn't even recognize—and twinkling, flashing, glowing lights *everywhere!*

"It's brighter than the dance club!" Jordan declared, shaking his head. His dark eyes twinkled, too, reflecting the red glare of the lights.

"He'll need a calculator to add up his electric bill!" I chimed in.

Everyone laughed. You see, Mr. Crowell is our math teacher. And he doesn't allow us to bring calculators to class.

Lenny scowled. "We should smash them," he muttered.

Mr. Crowell is *not* Lenny's favorite teacher.

In fact, Mr. Crowell isn't *anyone's* favorite teacher. Every school has at least one teacher that everyone hates. At Shadyside High, Mr. Crowell wins that prize.

I'm so easygoing and sensible, I get along well with all of my teachers. All except Mr. Crowell.

"Diane Browne, please complete this equation to the fifth decimal." I can hear his high, shrill voice. It always gives me chills, like chalk scraping on a blackboard.

I snuggled against Lenny. We were both glowing from the lights of the front yard. The tiny stud in Lenny's ear sparkled like a star. I kissed his cheek.

Poor Lenny. Mr. Crowell was toughest on him.

All the teachers were tough on Lenny. I guess because Lenny doesn't care much about school. Because he doesn't play the game. Because he's kind of tough looking.

Why do I go out with a guy like Lenny? A quiet, sensible girl like me?

Because I know him well enough to get past his surface cool. Because I know he's a really good guy underneath. He acts tough—but he's really a marshmallow.

Actually, I'm surprised that Lenny wants to go with *me*. I'm not as pretty as a lot of girls. I mean, I'm not as pretty as Cassie, for example. My blond hair is kind of scraggly and my nose is a little crooked. And I can't afford really neat clothes.

But Lenny and I have a good time together. When

he's not in one of his angry moods. Those times when he gets low, there isn't much I can do. Just wait for him to come out of it.

"I can't believe that a total *grump* like Crowell has so much Christmas spirit!" Cassie exclaimed.

"Did you ever see anything so ugly?" Jordan demanded, grinning. "I *love* it! I want to do this in *my* front yard. I'd keep it going all year!"

I laughed. Cassie shook her head disapprovingly. "You have no taste," she said softly.

"I know," Jordan shot back. "That's why I go out with *you!*"

Cassie shoved him into a hedge.

"No. I'm serious." Jordan grinned. "Mr. Crowell should win an award for this."

"He should be arrested," Lenny muttered bitterly.

Jordan laughed. "Excuse me? Arrested? For what?"

Lenny shrugged. "I don't know. Littering, maybe."

We laughed.

"I'm serious!" Lenny insisted. "I really think we should get my dad's Jeep, come back here, and drive it back and forth over all these stupid lights and Santas and reindeer. You know. Crunch them all to bits."

"Whoa," I murmured. I took Lenny's arm. "Take it easy," I whispered. "We *all* hate the guy. But——"

"Not as much as me," Lenny cried.

"Hey, we all have Crowell stories," Cassie chimed in. "Remember the time I lost my math notebook, and he dropped my grade a whole letter? And then I found the notebook at the bottom of my locker. I brought it in to show him—and he still wouldn't change my grade!" Cassie tossed back her coppery hair. "Remember that? And I'm his best student!"

"Remember when I got caught passing that note to

you?" I asked Lenny. "It was sort of a mushy love note. And Mr. Crowell grabbed it and called me up in front of everyone, and made me read it out loud?"

Just thinking about it made my face go hot. "That was the most embarrassing day of my life!" I declared. "I wanted to *murder* Mr. Crowell!"

"Me too," Lenny muttered.

Jordan tugged Cassie toward the street. "Let's get out of here. I'm getting a sunburn from all these lights!"

Lenny and I followed them across the street, then down the block. It took a while for my eyes to adjust to the darkness. None of the other houses was decorated.

A strong, cold breeze fluttered my hair. I pulled my down jacket tighter and snuggled against Lenny as we walked. "What time is it?" I yawned.

"Not too late. A little after midnight," he replied.

Up ahead of us, Cassie and Jordan were arguing again.

"I'm really tired." I sighed. "I worked all afternoon at the mall. Then it was so hot in the dance club . . ."

"That was fun," Lenny said, kicking a soda can across the street. "It felt good to kind of let go and just dance. You know?"

I nodded. "Yes, it did." I snickered. "Jordan thinks he's such a great dancer," I whispered. "But he works too hard at it, don't you think? He tries to be so cool, but—"

I stopped with a sharp gasp.

I saw something. A shadow. Something moving on the side of a house.

"Lenny—look!" I grabbed his arm.

He saw it too.

A dark figure. Climbing out of an upstairs window.

"He—he probably *robbed* the place!" I sputtered.

All four of us stared at the figure as he jumped to the ground.

"Quick—let's get out of here!" Cassie whispered.

Too late.

The burglar climbed quickly to his feet, spun around—and saw us.

chapter
2

Why didn't we run?

I'm not sure.

My heart was pounding, and my legs suddenly felt so rubbery. I'm not sure I *could* have run!

"Hey!" A hoarse cry escaped my throat as the figure ran toward us. He was dressed entirely in black—a black sweatshirt pulled down over black jeans. He had a black baseball cap pulled down low over his forehead, blocking his face from view.

Cassie shrank back beside me, her hands knotted in her coppery hair. Lenny and Jordan stepped forward, as if protecting us. But I could see the fear on their faces, too.

And then their expressions changed.

Lenny slapped the dark figure a high-five. Jordan cried out happily.

"Hey—Spencer!"

7

"Huh?" I choked out. I squinted into the pale light of a street lamp. And recognized Spencer Jarvis's surprised face.

"What are *you* doing here?" he demanded.

"What are *you* doing here?" I shot back.

He turned his gaze on me and smiled. "Hey, Diane—what's up?"

"I haven't seen you in almost a year!" I cried. I rushed forward and hugged him. He took off his baseball cap and returned the hug. His cheek felt burning hot against mine. Spencer and I had been really good friends. Until I started going with Lenny.

"Hey, Spencer—what's up with you?" Lenny stepped between us. He pointed to the house. "Why were you climbing out that window?"

"Wow," Jordan muttered. "Did you just rob that house?"

Spencer's grin grew wider, and he nodded. "Yeah. That's why you guys haven't seen me in school. I spend all my time robbing houses now."

I swallowed hard. Spencer had always been such a good guy.

"I'm rich," Spencer boasted. "I'm the best house burglar in Shadyside. In and out in a flash." He winked at me. "Never been caught. Never will be."

"But, Spencer—" Cassie gasped.

Spencer burst out laughing. "I'm putting you on."

"Huh?" Cassie and I both cried.

"Just joking," Spencer said. "You guys are still stupid, I see."

"Yeah. We're still stupid," Lenny agreed. He shook his head. "I never could tell when you were joking."

"You're not a burglar?" Jordan chimed in.

8

Spencer shook his head. "No way." He pointed. "That's my house. That's where we live now."

Lenny eyed him suspiciously. "You were climbing out of the bedroom window of your own house?"

Spencer nodded. "Yeah."

"How come?" I asked. "Why don't you use the door like most humans?"

"I'm not human. I'm an android," Spencer replied. It was never easy to get a straight answer from him. Sometimes he used to drive me crazy!

"I was sneaking out," he added. "Sometimes I like to sneak out after midnight." He grinned. "You know. Have some adventures. I call them Night Games."

"Games?" I asked.

"Don't your parents wonder—" Cassie started. Cassie was terrified of her parents. I couldn't imagine her ever daring to sneak out of the house.

"What my parents don't know won't hurt them," Spencer sneered.

I studied his face. He'd changed a lot in one year.

He had let his white-blond hair grow long, down to his shoulders and parted in the middle. His face had thinned, and he had a stubble of blond beard. Spencer had always been a little chubby. Now he looked muscular, athletic.

I saw that his black sweatshirt was inside out. Same old Spencer, I thought. He was always more than a little weird.

"What happened to you last year?" I asked him. "I called your house a million times. Then the phone company said the line had been disconnected."

He narrowed his pale eyes at me. "Didn't you get my letter?"

9

I shook my head. "No. I never got it."

I glimpsed a frown on Lenny's face. He never understood that Spencer and I were just friends. I think Lenny has always been a little jealous of Spencer.

"I sent it to explain why I left in such a hurry," Spencer continued. "Why I left without saying good-bye to anyone."

"Why?" Cassie asked.

"Well, you remember that my dad's store closed?" Spencer replied. "A few weeks after that, my grandmother in Washington got really sick. Well, she needed someone to take care of her after her operation. So, my dad decided to move us all to Washington. It was like a sudden thing."

"I remember your grandmother," I told Spencer. "Is she okay?"

He nodded. "Yeah. Pretty good. That's why we came back to Shadyside. My dad thought it would be easier to find work here." His silver-gray eyes locked on mine. "It's great to be home again. I missed you guys."

"Why haven't we seen you in school?" Jordan asked, pushing back his wavy, black hair.

"My parents sent me to St. Ann's," Spencer replied, lowering his eyes.

"Wow. Public school isn't good enough for you anymore, huh?" Lenny demanded. He meant it as a joke, but it didn't come out that way.

"I really did miss you guys," Spencer repeated. "Why don't you come along with me?"

"Come with you *where?*" Cassie asked suspiciously.

Spencer grinned. His eyes lit up. "For an adventure. A Night Game."

"What kind of adventure?" Lenny sneered. "You hunt for squirrels and bunny rabbits?"

Jordan laughed. "Yeah. What could be so thrilling in Shadyside?"

"Why don't you come find out?" Spencer challenged.

I turned to Cassie. She took a step back. Her arms were crossed in front of her parka, as if to protect herself. Cassie is not the adventurous type.

Neither am I. Besides, I was really tired from working all day and dancing all night.

But I didn't want Spencer to think I'm a wimp.

"What kind of adventure?" Lenny insisted.

"You don't do anything stupid, do you?" Cassie asked. A gust of wind fluttered her hair. She shivered. "I mean, you don't do anything illegal . . .?"

Spencer's grin widened. "I have adventures," he replied softly. "Some nights it's hard to sleep. My head feels so crowded. So I sneak out for some Night Games. Quiet little adventures . . . in the dark."

He turned, putting on his cap. Shoved his big hands into his jeans pockets. "You coming?"

I nodded to Cassie. She shrugged. Lenny and Jordan were already following Spencer.

"Yeah. I guess we're coming along," I said softly.

We followed Spencer down the dark street.

We didn't know it. But the Night Games had already begun for us.

And so had the terror.

chapter

3

We followed Spencer down the street. The houses were all dark. Street lamps made our shadows stretch eerily in front of us.

Cassie clung to Jordan as we walked. Lenny bobbed his head in rhythm as if listening to silent music. Our shoes crunched over newly fallen leaves.

None of us spoke. As we followed Spencer around the corner, I wondered if he knew where he was going. Or if he was just wandering.

What was he searching for?

He stopped suddenly, holding up both hands to signal for us to stop, too. Lenny and I stepped up beside him, and I saw where Spencer was staring.

At a white Taurus. Parked at the bottom of a driveway.

The windows were fogged, but the glare of a streetlight showed us the silhouettes of two people in the front seat.

A couple. Making out.

I saw a gleeful flash in Spencer's eyes. He raised a finger to his lips, motioning for us to be silent.

He pulled a flashlight from his back pocket. And tiptoed rapidly up to the car.

"What on earth . . .?" Cassie whispered.

Lenny and Jordan were both grinning. We followed Spencer. My heart started to thud.

Spencer stood over the car, too close for the boy and girl inside to see his face. Without warning, he pounded loudly on the driver's window. He pounded so hard, the car rocked from side to side.

"You're under arrest!" he bellowed. Spencer has a deep voice. He sounded very convincing, even to me.

We heard gasps and startled cries from inside the car. I saw the boy and girl pull apart.

Spencer aimed the flashlight into the window, flooding the car with light.

"Hey!" the boy inside cried.

"Come out with your hands raised!" Spencer ordered.

"What did we *do?* What did we *do?*" the girl shrieked.

"Officer, we were just leaving," the boy called out in a trembling voice.

"But I don't *get* it!" I heard the girl cry. "What did we *do?*"

"I'll think of something!" Spencer boomed.

The car door swung open, pushing Spencer back. A boy with spiky black hair started from the car.

Spencer shone the light in the boy's eyes. "Hey— you creep!" the boy protested.

Spencer placed the flashlight under his own chin. He twisted his face into a grimace and let out a long, evil laugh.

"You're dead meat!" the boy shouted furiously.

Spencer's evil grin grew wider. His eyes flashed excitedly. "Let's go!" he called to us.

Spencer spun around and started to run. His black cap flew off, but he didn't stop to pick it up.

I felt frozen to the spot. I wanted to get away from there. But I couldn't get my legs to cooperate.

Lenny grabbed my hand and tugged me off the grass. And before I realized it, we were running. All five of us. Running through the night. Our hair flying. Our shoes thudding heavily on the leaf-strewn pavement.

I glanced back and saw the boy and girl standing outside their car. The boy was shouting and shaking his fist at us.

But he didn't chase after us.

Lenny and Jordan congratulated Spencer as we ran. They slapped each other high-fives and celebrated as if they'd won some kind of victory.

Spencer tossed back his head and let out a long hyena wail.

Cassie and I glanced at each other, as if to say, What's the big deal?

I mean, all we did was terrify a boy and girl for a few seconds.

We didn't stop running until we reached Spencer's front yard. Then we all stopped to catch our breath.

Spencer let out another animal howl.

Lenny and Jordan laughed.

"Let's meet again," Spencer said breathlessly. He tugged back his white-blond hair with both hands. His chest heaved up and down. His eyes darted from one of us to another.

"Okay? How about it?" he demanded. "Monday after midnight? We'll all sneak out and have more adventures."

"I don't think so . . ." Cassie started.

But Lenny and Jordan eagerly agreed.

I didn't know what to say. I didn't really understand why they thought it was so much fun.

And something about Spencer's howls and the wild look on his face really worried me.

Why does he seem so excited? I wondered.

Why did he enjoy scaring that couple so much?

chapter

4

On Monday, we all sat in Mr. Crowell's math class. He stood at the chalkboard, scratching away at an algebra equation. Somehow the formula was supposed to measure the height of the school's flagpole.

I yawned. Mr. Crowell must be the most boring person on earth. The radiator by the window rattled. It was so hot. Everyone seemed ready for a nap.

Cassie sketched in her lab notebook. Her movements were slow, like Mr. Crowell's words.

I stared at a dark stain on the hem of my white sweater. I couldn't remember where it came from.

In front of me, Lenny and Jordan whispered to each other. That's when the trouble started.

Lenny snickered at something Jordan said. Mr. Crowell spun from the board so quickly that the chalk flew out of his hand. It smashed into the window and cracked in half.

Everybody jumped in surprise.

"Did that get your attention?" Mr. Crowell snarled at Lenny.

I watched Lenny's expression change. His smile faded quickly. Anger flashed in his dark brown eyes.

"Tell me, Lenny," Mr. Crowell said. "What was so funny? Do you find the equation humorous?"

Lenny snorted. "It's a riot."

I shut my eyes. *Please, Lenny,* I thought. *Just be quiet. Don't say anything. Don't get angry and get yourself in trouble again.*

"Is it a riot?" Mr. Crowell demanded. "Which part?"

The class fell silent. I shut my eyes tighter and crossed my fingers.

Lenny remained silent.

"I think you don't know which part is so funny," Mr. Crowell challenged. "I think you have no idea what's going on in this class."

Someone snickered. I opened my eyes in time to see Lenny sneer.

"Nothing to say?" Mr. Crowell challenged.

The back of Lenny's neck turned red. He stared hard at the teacher. I saw the muscles in his right cheek twitch.

I sank down in my seat. Mr. Crowell never knew when to stop. And he always knew how to push Lenny's buttons.

"No smart remark?" he teased Lenny. "I'm surprised. You find some way to disrupt this class every day. And now you don't have anything to say? What's wrong? Are you sick or something?"

A few kids laughed quietly. Cassie shot me a panicked glance.

"I didn't do anything," Lenny muttered.

"You haven't done anything all semester," the teacher snapped back.

I watched as a vein in Lenny's neck began to pulse. His eyes narrowed. He took a raspy breath and swung his legs out from under his desk.

Cassie leaned forward in her seat. I tensed, trying to think of some way to stop the coming explosion.

Lenny didn't move. But I saw him straining not to charge out of his seat. I knew he wanted to jump on the teacher and punch him out.

"I'm surprised you even bother with school," Mr. Crowell murmured, shaking his head. He turned back to the board, searching the grill for another piece of chalk.

The room remained silent.

Lenny rose slowly.

My whole body tingled. I wanted to say something—anything—to calm Lenny down. But my voice stuck in my throat.

Lenny knocked over the desk. It clattered hard on the wooden floor. Books and papers flew everywhere.

I gasped.

Glaring furiously at the teacher, Lenny took a step toward the front of the classroom.

Mr. Crowell turned from the blackboard to face him. "Sit down," he ordered.

I reached out my hand to grab Lenny's arm. "Lenny—no!" I whispered.

But he angrily shook my hand off. He balled his hands into fists and moved slowly toward Mr. Crowell.

I slid out of my seat. Tried to grab Lenny. Hold him. Pull him back.

Too late.

Lenny stepped up to Mr. Crowell and raised his fist.

"Lenny—don't!" I cried. "Don't!"

chapter
5

*L*enny froze. He turned to me. I met his eyes.

He took a shuddering breath and glanced down at his fists. His hands shook.

Then he let out a short angry cry, turned—and stomped out of the classroom.

Mr. Crowell stared at me. I lowered my eyes. I wondered if I should run after Lenny.

Jordan picked up Lenny's desk. I gathered up his papers and books.

As we cleaned, Mr. Crowell returned to the chalkboard and his algebra equation.

As though nothing had happened.

I shook my head unhappily. It wasn't fair that Mr. Crowell hated Lenny so much. He never gave Lenny a chance.

Lenny needed to be more careful. The teacher could

make things really bad for him. Last year, he got Lenny suspended from school twice.

One more suspension and Lenny would have to change schools.

I warned Lenny that he should keep quiet and do his assignments. But Lenny doesn't listen. Not even to his good, sensible girlfriend! He doesn't exactly look for trouble. But it always seems to find him.

Especially in Mr. Crowell's class.

I didn't even try to pay attention to the rest of the class. All I could think of was Lenny.

When the bell finally rang, I ran from the room. I knew that Lenny would be waiting by my locker. I hurried through the crowded hallway and ran upstairs.

No Lenny.

I dialed the combination and opened my locker. No note from Lenny. Where was he?

I turned to find Cassie leaning on the locker beside mine.

"Lenny needs to be careful, Diane," she said softly.

"Tell me something I don't know," I muttered, rolling my eyes.

"Mr. Crowell has a heart condition," Cassie continued. "I'm just afraid that one of these days, Lenny is going to give him a heart attack!"

"Good," I replied. We both laughed.

"He practically gives *me* a heart attack every day!" I joked.

Cassie frowned. "Are you still planning to sneak out after midnight tonight?" she asked. "Jordan thinks it's a really cool idea. I don't really want to. But if everyone else is doing it . . ."

I knelt down to search the bottom of my locker. "I

don't know what to do, either," I confessed. "If my parents caught me sneaking out after midnight, they'd *kill* me!"

Cassie nodded, biting her bottom lip thoughtfully.

I slammed the locker shut and turned to her. "I think I *will* sneak out tonight," I decided. "At least I'll have a chance to talk to Lenny."

Cassie nodded. "Okay. I'll go too. It's nice seeing Spencer again. Even though he's gotten a little weird."

"Yeah. Let's go," I repeated, convincing myself. "I mean, we're all just goofing, right? Having a little innocent fun. What could happen?"

chapter

6

Cassie and I met outside Spencer's house after midnight.

"Did you have trouble sneaking out?" I asked Cassie.

She nodded. "My parents stay up really late. I had to tiptoe downstairs and climb out the den window."

"I'm lucky," I replied. "My parents are heavy sleepers. Nothing wakes them. They once slept through an earthquake."

Cassie shivered and pulled her parka tight. It was a cold, raw night. The air felt more like winter than fall.

"Did you talk to Jordan and Lenny?" I asked her. "I tried calling Lenny all evening, but no one answered."

"I talked to Jordan," Cassie replied. "He said he'd bring Lenny."

We glanced up at Spencer's bedroom window. A

dim orange light glimmered in the room. But I didn't see any sign of Spencer.

A few seconds later, the tall evergreens beside the driveway shook. The brushing sound startled me. I turned—in time to see Jordan and Lenny come trotting up to us. White steam rose up from their mouths.

"Hey," Lenny muttered.

"Hey," Jordan echoed.

"How's it going, Diane?" Lenny asked.

I shrugged. "Where'd you go after school?"

"Just around," Lenny replied. "I don't know. I was so steamed. I just drove around."

Jordan slapped Lenny on the back. "When you knocked over your desk, I thought Crowell was going to jump out of his skin."

Lenny didn't smile.

"You've got to cool it in that class," I warned Lenny. "Maybe if you sit there like a statue, Crowell will ignore you."

"No way," Lenny replied angrily. "I'm not a good enough student for him to leave alone. Every chance he gets, he finds a way to get on my case. I never thought I could hate anyone as much as I hate that guy."

A soft scraping sound interrupted us. I gazed up to see Spencer's window slide open.

He waved at us, then quickly lowered himself down a rain gutter. "I *knew* you guys would come!" he exclaimed, grinning. "Everyone needs some Night Games from time to time—right?"

Spencer had his hair tied back in a thick ponytail. He wore a black sweatshirt—inside out—and baggy black chinos that were ripped at both knees.

He turned to Lenny. "How's it going?"

Lenny lowered his gaze to the ground. "I've been better."

"Crowell gave Lenny a hard time again in algebra," Jordan explained.

Spencer shook his head. "That jerk Crowell," he muttered with surprising anger. "He always gave me a hard time, too. I hate that guy."

"Let's not talk about it anymore," Cassie chimed in. "I mean, what are we *doing* out here? It's so cold. Why are we doing this?"

"Cheap thrills," Spencer replied, without smiling. "Let's go." He strode off so quickly, the four of us had to jog to catch up.

The air felt even colder. I pulled up the hood of my down jacket. Mist from the nearby river floated in and collected in the low spots near fences and hedges.

The whole world appeared so still. So unreal. Different . . . as if Shadyside were a different place late at night. Some kind of fantasy place of silvers and grays and long, black shadows.

Something darted from under a bush and scampered across our path. I screamed.

Cassie and Lenny laughed. "A killer chipmunk!" Cassie declared. More laughter, at my expense.

"Late at night, Shadyside is ours!" Spencer proclaimed.

Weird thought, I decided.

"The whole world belongs to us at night," Spencer added.

Lenny snickered. "Are you becoming some kind of poet or something?"

Spencer shook his head. "No way, Lenny. I'll become a poet when you become a math teacher!"

25

We all laughed at that, even Lenny.

I slid my arm around Lenny's waist and snuggled close to him as we made our way onto the next block. I had no idea where Spencer was leading us—until I saw the blaze of Christmas lights.

Mr. Crowell's house!

"Hey—why did we come back here?" Jordan demanded.

A grin spread over Spencer's face, but he didn't reply. He locked his eyes on the front window of the house.

"Let's keep moving," Lenny suggested impatiently. "I've had enough of this guy. Really."

Spencer turned his gaze on Lenny. "Maybe we can have some fun with him," he said softly. "Let's check Crowell out at home. You know. See if he has any dirty secrets."

"Huh? You mean *spy* on him?" I blurted out. I caught the worried expression on Cassie's face.

"Let's just take a look in there," Spencer replied. "You know. Peek in. See what Crowell does for laughs at night."

"But he'll see us!" Cassie protested. "This front yard is brighter than daylight!"

"We'll be careful," Spencer told her, his eyes trained on the house. "Come on. Quick."

He moved silently over the wet grass toward the house, stepping around lights and decorations. We followed him, then ducked down behind a round bush that grew in front of the living room window.

"If he looks out the window, he'll see us," Cassie warned. She shivered.

A gust of cold air made me shiver, too.

What am I doing here? I asked myself. After mid-

26

night on a school night, crouched in front of a teacher's window?

It's crazy—but kind of exciting, I admitted to myself.

We raised our heads over the bush and peeked into the window. The lights were on, but turned down low. I could hear Christmas music playing.

Against the back wall, I saw Mr. Crowell stringing silver garlands on a Christmas tree. He's working on his tree really late, I thought. Most teachers I know go to bed early because they have to get up so early.

Squinting into the dimly lit room, I saw four open boxes on the couch. They were propped on their sides and full of ornaments.

"Nothing like rushing the season," Lenny muttered. "What's *with* this guy, anyway?"

"He doesn't have kids or a family or anything," Jordan added. "He's doing all this Christmas stuff for himself."

"Weird," Lenny said under his breath.

"Shh," Cassie warned. "He'll hear us."

We watched Mr. Crowell trim his tree for another few minutes. Then he turned out the living room lamps to enjoy the sparkle of his decorations. He sat down in an armchair, drank from a can of soda, and stared at his creation with a satisfied expression.

"Bor-ing!" I declared. "All he's doing is staring at his ugly tree." I turned to Spencer. "This isn't much of an adventure."

"Yeah. Let's go," Lenny agreed. "I see enough of this creep during the day. I don't want to watch him at night, too."

Lenny tugged me away from the bush. Cassie and Jordan followed us. We edged away from the window and started to make our way down the gravel driveway.

I thought Spencer was right behind us.

But a loud crash made me spin around.

"Whoa!" I cried out when I saw Spencer swing his big flashlight. He smashed it into a cluster of twinkling red and green lights.

The lights crackled as they broke.

Spencer tugged out a section of lights by the wires. Then he stomped on a lighted Santa. The Santa cracked and toppled over. Spencer kicked it across the lawn.

"Hey—stop it!" I screamed.

"Spencer—what are you *doing?*" Jordan cried.

Spencer ignored us. He pulled out more lights.

Then he pulled an aluminum reindeer from the ground—and heaved it toward the house.

"Spencer—stop!" Cassie and I screamed.

Spencer was like a wild man. He was swinging his flashlight, smashing lights, grunting with each swing, his eyes wild, his mouth open.

"Let's get *out* of here!" I cried.

Too late.

The porch light flashed on. The front door opened.

And Mr. Crowell stepped onto the stoop. "I see you!" he screamed.

chapter

7

Cold panic washed over me. I let out a gasp. Then I lowered my head and ran.

All five of us were running hard. Our shoes thudded on the pavement. It sounded like a cattle stampede.

I could hear the teacher screaming angrily from his stoop. His voice was high and shrill on the heavy night air.

I didn't turn back.

Had he really seen us? Had he recognized us?

Lenny is so tall. I'll bet he recognized Lenny, I thought.

The front lawn was so bright, he *had* to have seen us! I decided, feeling a chill of dread.

Cassie stumbled into Jordan but quickly regained her balance. Spencer led the way, running hard, waving his flashlight high in front of him.

A thousand pictures flashed through my mind as I

followed him, running so hard my side started to ache.

I pictured the police at my front door, dragging me away as my parents watched in horror.

I pictured myself trying to explain to my parents why I was out in the middle of the night, destroying Mr. Crowell's Christmas display.

I pictured Mr. Crowell standing over me, accusing me. Accusing all of us. I saw Mr. Hernandez, the principal, handing me my records file, telling me I could never go to Shadyside High again.

Horrible, frightening pictures.

And then, as I shook them from my mind, I heard laughter.

I felt so startled, I nearly stopped running.

I heard laughter. Spencer's laughter. Gleeful laughter.

"That was *awesome!*" he cried, waving his flashlight high. "Awesome!"

And then Lenny and Jordan were laughing, too.

"Did you see the look on Crowell's face?"

"He went as red as the reindeer's nose!"

"Happy holidays, Mr. Crowell!"

"And Happy New Year!"

The boys were laughing and congratulating each other, slapping Spencer on the back, hooting and shouting loudly. Too loudly. I glanced around, wondering if we were waking up people in the nearby houses.

Once again, we stopped in front of Spencer's house. Two large gray cats stared at us from the driveway. They tilted their heads as if trying to figure out why five teenagers were out so late.

"Spencer—that was horrible!" Cassie scolded. She gasped in air, trying to catch her breath.

"You loved it!" Spencer shot back gleefully.

"It was horrible!" Cassie repeated.

"It was awesome!" Spencer argued.

Lenny turned to me with a grin on his face. "Wish I had a camera," he said softly.

"What if he saw us?" Cassie demanded.

"No way," Spencer insisted. "He could only see our backs."

"He could never prove it," Lenny added. "Even if he saw us. Even if he suspects it was us. He has no proof."

"Right," Jordan agreed. "We were all home safe and sound in our beds, right?"

"I thought we weren't going to do illegal things," Cassie said angrily.

"Yeah. You should have warned us," I told Spencer.

He didn't reply. "When do you guys want to go out again?" he asked. "Tomorrow night?"

"Huh? Go out again?" Cassie cried.

Spencer nodded. "How about tomorrow night?"

"Excellent!" Lenny exclaimed. "What do you say, Diane?"

I swallowed hard. My throat felt dry. My heart still raced from our long run.

"Only on one condition," I replied. I turned to Spencer. "You have to warn us before you do anything crazy," I told him.

"No problem," he said. He grinned and scratched his white-blond hair.

"Do you mean it?" I insisted. "No more surprises?"

His grin grew wider. "I promise," he said, raising his right hand. "Cross my heart and hope to die."

chapter

8

*L*enny dropped me off at my house. I crept inside, trying to be totally silent.

But when I reached my bedroom, the phone was ringing. I dove across the bed and grabbed the receiver.

"Hello?" I whispered.

"Diane, it's Bryan."

Bryan Hedges. He's the guy I broke up with last winter when I decided I wanted to go out with Lenny.

Lately Bryan had been pestering me about getting back together.

I felt bad that I had hurt Bryan's feelings. And I have to admit, I was flattered to have two guys interested in me.

But I didn't want to go out with Bryan anymore.

And I certainly didn't want him calling me in the middle of the night.

"It's too late to be calling, Bryan," I whispered. I glanced at my alarm clock. "What is your problem? It's nearly three in the morning. My parents will take away my phone if you woke them up."

"Sorry," he whispered back. "I just wanted to talk. You know."

"Well, I can't talk now," I shot back angrily. "Really, Bryan. I don't want you calling. I—"

"We really should talk," Bryan insisted. "I mean, maybe Friday night after the basketball game . . ."

"No way!" I interrupted. "Give me a break, okay? You know I'm going with Lenny now."

"Lenny is a jerk," Bryan muttered. "You and I—"

"Good night, Bryan," I groaned. "I'm hanging up now. And don't call again. I mean it."

Bryan's voice suddenly turned menacing. "You'll be sorry," he said.

"Excuse me?"

"You'll be sorry, Diane," he repeated, "if you keep seeing Lenny."

"Is that a threat?" I cried shrilly. "Bryan, have you totally lost it?"

I didn't wait for him to reply. I slammed the phone down.

My heart was pounding. My hands were balled into tight fists. I felt so angry, I wanted to scream.

What right did Bryan have to call me in the middle of the night and make ugly threats?

"Oh!"

I cried out as the phone rang again.

I grabbed the receiver angrily and raised it to my ear. "Bryan, I'm warning you—"

"Diane, I saw you tonight," a whispered voice rasped.

"Bryan—stop it!" I cried.

"I saw you tonight, Diane. I know about your Night Games," the voice whispered.

"Get off the phone, Bryan!" I cried. "You're not funny. It's you—right? Bryan? Bryan?"

Last Winter

chapter

9

Spencer drew a deep breath as he turned the old car into his uncle's driveway. The ski cabin stood at the end of a long, winding mountain road, and Spencer had missed too many curves on the way up.

I'm lucky I didn't skid off a cliff in this piece-of-junk car, he thought. Why don't they put guardrails on those turns?

He was still shaking from the dangerous drive. But now that he had arrived, he could relax. He waited for Diane, Lenny, Cassie, and Jordan to join him for the weekend.

His uncle promised that there was plenty of food at the cabin, and wood for a roaring fire. Cable TV. And his uncle's artificial Christmas tree waiting to be decorated.

Spencer couldn't wait for his friends to show up.

After last night's snowfall, the slopes would be perfect. Everyone would be impressed by his uncle's cabin. The only way the weekend could be better was if he had a girlfriend with him.

Spencer hated being the only one without a girl-friend.

His friends thought he was shy. They always teased him about it. Especially Lenny.

They didn't get it.

Spencer knew he could find someone to date. But he was picky about who he went out with. She had to be smart, pretty, and fun. Someone perfect.

Someone like Diane.

Thinking about Diane, Spencer scowled.

When Diane broke up with Bryan, Spencer thought for sure she would go out with him. They had been friends for years, and he knew Diane liked him. But Spencer had waited too long. Lenny asked Diane out first.

And then it was Diane and Lenny, together all the time.

Spencer climbed out of the old car and waved at the headlights of Jordan's Jeep. Jordan came from a rich family.

It must be nice to get cars as birthday presents, Spencer thought. The last birthday present he got was a pair of out-of-style sneakers from his dad's store.

As Jordan pulled into the snow-covered driveway, he gunned the engine. The wheels picked up snow, flinging it over Spencer. It whipped into his face, stung his cheeks, and soaked the fur hood of his parka.

Spencer groaned and wiped the water from his eyes.

He saw Diane and Cassie in the backseat. They pointed at him, giggling.

Jordan jumped out of the Jeep. "Hey—my aim is getting better!" he declared, laughing.

Lenny climbed out next. "Yo, Spence!" he called. "We saw your car leaning too far to the left. Maybe you should cut down on the Snickers bars!"

The joke angered Spencer. So *what* if he was a little chubby? Who gave Lenny the right to make fun of him in front of Diane?

Lenny is a jerk, Spencer decided angrily. A total jerk.

Diane climbed out of the Jeep and began pulling bags from the back. Spencer watched in silence. He had tried to convince Diane that her new boyfriend was bad news. But Diane told him she didn't need his advice.

The worst part was that she brought Lenny with her everywhere. To the movies. To Pete's Pizza. To the mall.

To Spencer's uncle's cabin.

"Hey—this is excellent!" Cassie's voice interrupted Spencer's thoughts. "Thanks for inviting us."

Spencer felt a little better. Cassie could always cheer him up. "No problem," he said softly. He stepped over to the girls and slung an arm around each of them.

He watched Lenny stiffen as he passed by. It made him smile. "Let's get a fire started," Spencer suggested to Diane and Cassie.

He pulled open the cabin door. Dark. And very cold. Spencer searched for the wall switch and flooded the place with light.

His uncle's cabin was beautiful. With a wide, stone

fireplace, a wall of floor-to-ceiling windows, and a cozy loft.

"How pretty!" Diane exclaimed. She studied the room as she pulled off her gloves and ski cap.

"Whoa!" Jordan cried as he dropped his backpack onto the living room couch. "Your uncle must have some major bucks. Check out the stereo system!"

"I always knew your uncle Jarvis was loaded!" Lenny agreed. "Hey, Spence, how about a loan?"

Diane shoved him playfully. "Give Spencer a break," she scolded.

Yeah. Give Spencer a break, Spencer thought bitterly. Take a long walk in the snow, Lenny. And don't come back.

"Spencer," Cassie called. "It's freezing in here. Building a fire was a good idea."

Spencer nodded. "Sure. I'll have it warm in here in a few minutes."

He pointed down the hallway. "The cabin has three bedrooms. You have your choice. Go settle in while I build the fire."

His friends disappeared, checking out all the rooms.

Spencer carefully stoked a flame in the fireplace. He concentrated on building the fire.

But a few seconds later, Lenny's angry voice from down the hall broke into Spencer's thoughts. "Stop telling me what to do, Diane!" Lenny warned. "I didn't want to come up here in the first place. I came along for you."

"You didn't have to," Spencer heard Diane reply. "You don't have to follow me around everywhere I go."

"You follow me. I don't follow you," Lenny insisted.

Spencer heard Jordan step into the argument. "Will you guys give it a rest? We're supposed to have fun this weekend."

Spencer heard some muttered words. He couldn't make them out. He heard Lenny mention his name. Then he heard Jordan laugh.

Are they laughing at me? Spencer wondered.

Spencer felt his cheeks turn red. Before Lenny joined their group, Jordan had been a really good friend. Was Jordan laughing at him now?

Diane and Cassie drifted back into the living room, talking quietly. Spencer bent over the fire. He didn't want them to know he had heard them.

Two large, green leather sofas faced each other in the middle of the room. The couples paired off and plopped down on them. Immediately they flipped on the wide-screen television.

Lenny wanted to see the hockey match. Jordan wanted to watch one of the *Lethal Weapon* movies. The girls wanted to tune in to a figure-skating competition.

Spencer sat on the floor and kept quiet. He knew Lenny would get his way. Lenny always got his way.

A loud howl burst through the cabin.

The back door blew open in the sudden wind and slammed against the wall.

The lights flickered once. Then the entire cabin went dark.

For a moment nobody spoke.

Then Lenny groaned. "Oh, great," he said with a sigh. "A power failure."

"No problem," Spencer announced. "We've got candles and lanterns."

"Do you have a candle-powered TV?" Jordan joked.

Spencer ignored him. He climbed up from the rug and walked into the kitchen for the propane lantern.

It took him a while to find it in the dark. Then he lugged it back to the coffee table and lit it. The room flickered with orange light.

"There. That's better." Spencer glanced at Lenny and saw an angry scowl on his face. Diane crossed her arms and stared straight ahead.

An argument. They must have fought while he was out of the room.

"I didn't want to come here in the first place, Diane," Lenny muttered. "Why do I let you convince me to do stuff like this?"

He stared right at Spencer as he spoke. As if he didn't care at all about Spencer's feelings.

Diane slid away from Lenny on the couch. "I'm really sick of your complaining," she snapped. "You're acting like a baby. If it's so bad in here, why don't you go out and sit in the car?"

Spencer almost laughed out loud. He loved seeing Lenny blow it. Maybe Diane would dump Lenny this weekend.

Lenny leapt to his feet. "Fine!" he snarled. "If you want me, I'll be in the Jeep." He grabbed his coat and stomped outside, slamming the cabin door behind him.

"Don't you think you should go after him?" Cassie asked Jordan.

Jordan shook his head. "He'll be back before you

know it—it's freezing out! He just needs to blow off some steam. It will be the best thing for all of us."

"What's his problem, anyway?" Spencer asked, sitting beside Diane.

"School," Jordan answered. "What else?"

"Can't we talk about something besides Lenny?" Cassie interrupted. "I'm sure Diane would appreciate it."

Spencer shifted his gaze to Diane. "You okay?"

She shrugged. "Yeah. Fine." She turned her gaze to the orange flames dancing in the fireplace.

A couple of minutes later, Jordan and Cassie snuggled close on their couch. They kissed. A long, passionate kiss.

Diane stared straight ahead, acting as if she didn't notice. But it made Spencer uncomfortable. He decided to get some wood from the shed. "I'm going to bring in some more logs for the fire," he explained.

"Can I come with you?" Diane asked softly.

"Sure," he answered.

She hurried to get her coat from the bedroom. They left Cassie and Jordan kissing on the couch.

Spencer held Diane's arm as they tramped through the snow. When they reached the shed where his uncle stored the firewood, he paused to light another lantern hanging from a peg.

He saw Diane shiver. She glanced at the thick evergreens crowding around the shed.

Spencer loaded kindling sticks while Diane took a seat on the chopping block. She sighed. "I thought Cassie and Jordan were bad," she murmured, keeping her eyes on the trees.

"What do you mean?" Spencer asked.

"You know. Fighting all the time. But now, Lenny and I . . ." Her voice trailed off.

"What's his problem, anyway?" Spencer demanded.

Diane sighed. "I don't know," she answered. "I really don't. Sometimes we get along great. But sometimes he's just impossible. Like tonight."

She stopped to brush her straight, blond hair from her eyes.

"He's always losing it," she continued. "Especially when we're not doing what Lenny wants to do."

"He has to run the show, huh?" Spencer asked.

She nodded. And looked so sad that he dropped the sack of sticks to come over to her. He tenderly cupped her chin in his hand and gazed into her soft brown eyes.

Diane blinked and smiled.

Before he realized what he was doing, Spencer leaned toward Diane. Slowly. Until their faces touched.

Until their lips touched.

A hand grabbed Spencer's shoulder roughly.

Spun him around.

He stared into Lenny's angry face.

Spencer opened his mouth. But he didn't have time to say anything.

Lenny punched him hard in the mouth.

The pain seared through Spencer's jaw. He stumbled back.

He stared at Lenny. Stunned. Felt warm blood trickle down his chin.

Lenny came for him again.

But Diane stepped between them. "That's enough!" she cried. "Lenny—have you gone *crazy?*"

Lenny tried to push past her. She threw her slight weight against him, long enough to force him to stop.

"Stay away from Diane!" Lenny screamed. "Or you'll be sorry! You'll be sorry!"

Spencer stared at Lenny, feeling his anger rise.

He lowered his gaze to the snow. Saw the blood from his cut mouth puddling darkly at his feet.

Dark blood on the white, white snow. Glowing in the lantern light.

When Spencer raised his eyes, Lenny was dragging Diane back to the cabin.

Spencer felt his fury build.

This isn't right, Lenny, he thought. Not right at all. You can't treat people this way.

I can't let you get away with this.

I *can't*.

This Winter

chapter
10

Cassie and I went to Pete's Pizza after school on Tuesday. She insisted we try the Vegetarian Surprise pizza. We ordered a large pie. But as soon as we started eating, I wished I had ordered our usual pepperoni. It wouldn't have been as healthy. But at least I wouldn't be picking off chunks of half-cooked carrot every few seconds.

"Diane, you look so stressed out," Cassie remarked, wiping cheese off her chin.

I sighed. "Sorry. I was just thinking about Bryan."

Cassie's mouth opened in shock. "Huh? Bryan? What about Bryan?"

"He called me last night," I told her. I pulled off a chunk of crust and nibbled at it.

Cassie stared at me. "You're kidding! What did he want?"

"To get back together. What else does Bryan ever want?"

She leaned across the table. "Well, what did you tell him?"

I sighed. "I told him it wasn't going to happen."

"Did he believe you?"

"I don't know, Cassie. Then he got weird. He started threatening me. Telling me I would be sorry if I stayed with Lenny. He started whispering, saying that he knew about our Night Games."

Cassie let her pizza slice drop to her plate. "Huh? How would he know about that?"

I shrugged. "I don't have time to worry about Bryan. I have bigger things to worry about. Like Lenny."

"Are you two having problems?" Cassie asked.

"Not really," I replied. "I'm just worried about him. He's so angry all the time. I'm scared he'll lose it one of these times and do something really bad."

"He has been getting into trouble at school a lot," Cassie agreed.

"Yeah," I answered. "It's something different every day." I shoved my plate away. "But I know Lenny is a good guy. If people would just give him a break . . ."

We sat in silence for a moment. Cassie picked at her pizza. I sipped my Coke. Then we chatted about the Night Games.

"Spencer has changed a lot in a year," Cassie remarked.

"He still wears his sweatshirts inside out," I joked.

"But everything else about him has changed," Cassie insisted. "He used to be . . . well . . . sort of a wimp. Now he seems so confident, so self-assured."

"He's a lot more fun," I admitted. "Although he's

kind of scary sometimes. I mean, you get the feeling that he'll do anything. You know. Just for the adventure. I mean—"

I stopped when I saw Lenny burst into the restaurant.

He staggered through the door, bumped against the first booth. Then, spotting us, he hurtled forward.

"Lenny . . .?" I started.

His face was bright red, his features twisted.

As he lurched toward us, he held his right hand.

"Oh!" I cried out as I saw the blood dripping from his hand.

"Lenny—" I cried. "Lenny—what's wrong?"

"*D*iane, I—I—"

Lenny dropped beside me in the booth. He grabbed a handful of napkins from the dispenser, wadded them up, and dabbed at his bleeding hand.

"What happened to your hand?" I demanded shrilly.

"Mr. Crowell happened to my hand," he replied angrily.

"Huh? What are you talking about?" Cassie asked.

"You didn't hit Mr. Crowell—did you?" I inquired.

Lenny shook his head impatiently. "No. I wish I had! I cut my hand on my locker."

Relief flooded through me. "You punched your locker?" I guessed.

"Yeah," he answered bitterly. "I was so furious, I couldn't think straight."

"What did Crowell do this time?" I whispered.

"He got me kicked off the basketball team," Lenny replied, dabbing at his cut hand.

"Oh, no!" I knew how much the basketball team meant to Lenny. "How?"

"Because of my grades," he mumbled. "It's the same old story with him. He hates me. He always tries to ruin things for me. He went to the coach and told him I was failing algebra."

"Oh, wow," I muttered, shaking my head.

Cassie tsk-tsked.

"I can't let him do this to me," Lenny said heatedly. "I can't let him ruin my life. I mean, the season hasn't even started yet, and he already got me kicked off the team!"

"Why don't you go in tomorrow and try talking to him?" I suggested.

He made a disgusted face. "You don't get it, Diane. Crowell doesn't want to talk to me. He wants to get me thrown out of school."

"It's not that bad," I protested.

"Hey, guys!"

I glanced up to see Jordan slide in beside Cassie. He smoothed his wavy, dark hair, then dipped into the pizza pan.

"Tough luck, Lenny," he said. "I heard Crowell went to the coach today."

"News travels fast," Lenny muttered bitterly.

"The whole team knows by now," Jordan reported.

He studied his slice of pizza with a small frown. He glanced at Cassie. "You ordered this, didn't you?"

"What's wrong with it?" she asked.

"Why can't you just order plain old pepperoni for once?" he asked. "Why does it always have to be this weird, lumpy stuff?"

He held the slice out for Lenny to inspect. "See that?" he said, pointing to an artichoke heart. "Mutant food toppings."

Lenny angrily pushed the slice from his face. "Give me a break, Jordan," he snarled.

"Hey—give *me* a break!" Jordan snapped back.

"Take it easy, guys," I warned.

"Yeah. Take it easy," Jordan agreed, staring at Lenny. "Let's talk about something else, okay?"

"Good idea," Cassie said quickly.

"Are we sneaking out tonight?" Jordan asked. "Are we meeting Spencer after midnight?"

"I . . . I guess so," I replied uncertainly. I turned to Lenny. He had the strangest expression on his face.

"Yes. Tonight," he said thoughtfully. "We're sneaking out after midnight. And tonight . . . no smashed lights or decorations. Tonight we're *really* going to get Mr. Crowell."

chapter
12

I know, I know.

I'm Diane Browne. I'm supposed to be the sensible, practical one in our group.

So why did I go along with these Night Games of Spencer's? And why didn't I argue with Lenny when he said he wanted us to return to Mr. Crowell's house and get revenge on him?

It's hard to explain.

I suppose I was as caught up in the excitement of the Night Games as everyone else. It was kind of thrilling to sneak out of the house, to walk around the neighborhood when no one else was awake. To be able to go anywhere we pleased and not be seen by anyone.

Freedom. That's what it was. An exciting kind of freedom that made our skin tingle, made our senses more alert, made our hearts pound a little faster.

When you stop to think about it, we don't have much freedom during the day.

There is always someone around to tell us where we have to be and what we have to do. Always someone to say, "Go to school. Do your homework. Help your brother. Do your chores. Go to the store. Go to bed."

After midnight, roaming the silent sidewalks and yards of Shadyside, *we* were in charge.

No one to tell us to turn left, turn right, cross the street.

The world belonged to us.

That was part of it. The other part was Spencer.

He had changed so much in a year. Not just his appearance.

Yes, he had slimmed down. His face was slender and intense now. His body no longer chubby and weak looking, but athletic and light.

Something about his eyes . . .

I can't really describe it. Spencer had always been a nice guy, kind of wimpy, not much on personality. Sort of a steady, dependable, uninteresting kind of guy.

But now he could make you follow him with just a smile or a word. I guess that somehow he had become a leader. Not that he was bossy or pushy. He never tried to push us around.

He just seemed so . . . confident.

As if he knew exactly what he was doing. As if he knew exactly what he wanted.

And he wanted to have adventures late at night. Nothing heavy duty. Nothing evil.

Just adventures.

At least, that's what I thought—until the night

Lenny insisted we return to Mr. Crowell's house. That night, it all shot out of control.

That's the night we lost it. For good.

It was a raw, cold November night. A solid frost hardened the ground and made the lawns shimmer like silver.

I sneaked out the back door a few minutes after midnight and hurried to our meeting place in Spencer's backyard. My breath steamed up above me as I jogged across the yards. I hadn't bothered to zip my heavy down coat. It flapped noisily behind me as I ran.

I was the first to arrive. I ducked down behind a low evergreen shrub and peered up at Spencer's bedroom window. Solid black. The entire house stood in darkness.

A few moments later, Cassie and Jordan appeared. They seemed to be arguing—as usual. I couldn't catch what it was about. They stopped as soon as they saw me.

"Where's Spencer?" Jordan demanded impatiently.

I shrugged. "He didn't climb out yet." I turned to Cassie. She had her coppery hair tucked under a black wool cap. "How are you?"

She shivered and rubbed the sleeves of her parka. "Cold."

"Is Lenny really going to take us back to Crowell's?" Jordan demanded.

"Yeah. Why not?" a familiar voice interrupted. Lenny hunched down beside us. He wore his maroon-and-gray Shadyside Tigers basketball team jacket.

I swallowed hard. I wanted to hug him. I knew how bad Lenny felt about being removed from the team.

"Where's Spencer? He's late," Lenny complained. He gazed tensely at his watch. "It's nearly twelve-thirty."

We all stared up at the dark window. No sign of anyone or anything.

"I brought my cell phone," Jordan said, reaching into his pocket. "Let's call him and—"

"Put that away!" Cassie cried. "You'll wake up his parents!"

"Oh. Right." Jordan slid the little phone back into his pocket.

"We could throw little rocks at his window," I suggested. "That's what they always do in the movies."

"Too risky," Cassie said. "If we break a window . . ."

"Maybe he forgot about us," Jordan suggested, frowning.

"How could he forget the Night Games?" Lenny snapped. "They're *his* idea."

"You don't have to jump down my throat, Lenny!" Jordan cried.

"Shhhh." I stepped between the two boys. "You're going to wake up the whole neighborhood."

"Well, it's too cold to wait out here much longer," Cassie said, shivering. "Let's go."

"We've *got* to wait for him," Lenny insisted.

"Maybe you do. But I don't!" Cassie shot back.

"You're a whole bunch of fun," Jordan told her, rolling his eyes sarcastically.

"Please!" I whispered. "Everybody just stop." I

gazed up at Spencer's window. "Let's give him two more minutes. Then . . ."

Spencer stepped out from the side of the house and signaled to us with a wave. The four of us scurried out from behind the bush to greet him.

Once again, he wore a black sweatshirt over black denim jeans. He had a black ski cap pulled down over his white-blond hair.

"Where were you?"

"We thought you forgot about us."

"It's so cold. We were going to leave."

He motioned with both hands for us to calm down. "Sorry, guys. I fell asleep." He shrugged. "I was studying, and I fell asleep." He glanced from one of us to the next. "What's up?"

"I want to go back to Crowell's," Lenny told him eagerly. Lenny's dark eyes lit up excitedly. "Tonight I want to do some damage. Some *real* damage."

"Whoa!" Spencer cried. "Hold on, Lenny."

"Yeah. Hold on," Cassie chimed in. "We want to have fun. We don't want to get in trouble."

Lenny groaned. "I really need to get this guy, Spencer," he pleaded. "Tonight, let's smash the rest of his lights. Let's—"

Spencer grabbed Lenny by the shoulders. "Whoa. Whoooa."

"Hey—back off!" Lenny pulled away angrily. He scowled at Spencer. "This stuff was all your idea, man. Now you're going to wimp out?"

"No way," Spencer insisted. "But these Night Games aren't about revenge, Lenny. They're about having fun."

"That's what I'm saying," Lenny replied, breathing hard. "Let's have fun by getting revenge!"

Lenny was so earnest, so totally serious, we all had to laugh. Even Spencer.

Lenny's expression remained intense. "Hey, I know you and I didn't always get along," he told Spencer, lowering his gaze to the ground. "I mean, we had some rough times. I remember. But that was a long time ago—right? And now you're *with* me—right?"

Spencer glanced at me, then at Cassie. Then he turned toward the street without answering Lenny. "Let's go, guys," Spencer said softly. "It's getting very late."

As we trotted after him, I wondered what Spencer was thinking. Was he sorry that he invited us to come along on his Night Games? Were we ruining the whole thing for him?

Did he want to help Lenny get his revenge on Mr. Crowell?

Spencer and Jordan had been pretty good friends at one time. But Lenny and Spencer had never gotten along well at all. Had Spencer forgotten all about the old days?

He seemed so changed, I bet that he *had* forgotten all the unhappiness of the past.

We stopped across the street from Mr. Crowell's house. To our surprise, the lights in the front yard had all been turned off. Darkness washed over the house and yard. The metal reindeer and sleighs glimmered dully in the pale moonlight.

No lights on in the house.

"Weird," Lenny muttered. "Crowell usually stays up late."

We crossed the street and made our way quickly, silently, up the driveway. Spencer peeked into the open garage. "Car is gone," he reported. "Mr. Crowell must be out."

"Weird," Lenny repeated. "On a school night?"

Spencer peeked into a side window. Jordan grabbed the stone window ledge and lifted himself up to peer into the living room window.

"No one home," Spencer whispered. A grin spread over his face. He slapped Lenny's shoulder. "Your lucky night, man."

Lenny grinned back at him. "What are we going to do?" He motioned to the front yard. "Get to work on the Christmas decorations?"

"No way," Spencer replied. He turned to glance at the house next door. Also completely dark. Then he turned back to the side window.

What does Spencer have in mind? I wondered.

Why is he grinning like that? Why does he look so excited?

He raised both hands to the frame of the side window. And he gave a hard push.

The window slid up easily.

"Come on, guys," Spencer whispered, hoisting himself up. "We're going in."

chapter

13

"**S**pencer!" Cassie hissed. "What are you doing?"

He had already disappeared inside the house. So she turned to me. "We can't do this, Diane," she moaned. "What if we get caught?"

"If we get caught, we'll tell him we came over for extra math credit," Lenny joked. With a grunt, he raised himself through the open window.

"Diane!" Cassie whispered frantically. "This is crazy! It really is!"

I knew Cassie was right. I also knew we could all get in major trouble. But as I said, I felt too excited to be sensible. I was just caught up in the whole thing. Caught up by the craziness of it.

"Cassie, stay out here if you want," I murmured, and followed the two boys inside.

Cassie stood still for a minute before crawling in

behind us. "This is a huge mistake," she repeated in a trembling voice. "A huge mistake."

Jordan slid in behind her, blinking, waiting for his eyes to adjust to the darkness.

"Let's do some damage!" Lenny cried happily. He found a switch on the wall and flicked on the light.

"Noo!" Spencer cried and and slapped the switch back down. "Are you out of your mind?" he growled. "What if a neighbor sees the light? What if Crowell gets home and sees a light on?"

"Yeah. You're right. Sorry," Lenny muttered.

We crept around Mr. Crowell's house for a few minutes. The wooden floorboards squeaked and creaked beneath our shoes.

Moonlight shone through the living room window, reflecting off the furniture. The living room was cluttered, jammed with electronics. I saw a computer and printer, a big television set. And a nice stereo. Lots of CDs.

"Spencer, are we just going to creep around? What are we going to do?" I demanded in a harsh whisper. "It's late. Mr. Crowell could come home any second."

"Let's trash the place," Lenny suggested.

Jordan gasped and spun around. "No way!" he cried. "We can't trash the place. That's a serious crime, Lenny."

"I have a better idea," Spencer announced. "Let's just move a few things around."

"Huh? What good is that?" Lenny demanded.

"It's a great idea!" I chimed in. "If we just move a couple of items, Mr. Crowell will know someone was in here. He'll freak out!"

"Yeah. He'll totally freak," Spencer agreed. "But he won't have any real reason to call the police."

It sounded harmless to me. Even Cassie agreed.

Spencer crossed the room to the Christmas tree. He pulled the star off the top and set it on the mantel.

Lenny snickered. He grabbed an arm of the couch and tugged the couch around until it faced a wall.

Jordan switched around a couple of pictures in the hallway. He hung one upside down.

Giggling, Cassie tied a pair of window curtains together. Then she turned on the computer.

I didn't touch anything. Instead, I explored the rest of the house. Mr. Crowell had good taste. The kitchen was filled with shiny new appliances. Expensive-looking pots and pans hung from hooks in the ceiling. A tall vase stuffed with silk flowers sat on the kitchen table.

I walked down a short hallway to check out the bathroom. This room didn't have a window, so I chanced turning on the light by the medicine cabinet.

The shower curtain pictured Bugs Bunny and Daffy Duck. I burst out laughing. Nasty Mr. Crowell, a closet cartoon-watcher? I couldn't believe it.

I left the light on and shut the door behind me. That would give him something to think about!

Out in the hallway, the only light came from the moon shining through the living room windows. I trailed my fingers along the wall as I walked, letting my eyes grow used to the shadows.

So dark. And quiet.

I moved along the back hall. Found myself in a small bedroom at the back of the house.

I should get back, I thought. Why did I wander back here? I can't hear my friends.

I started toward the door—when I saw the dark figure stretched out on the bed.

I saw the long legs first. Then the arms, sprawled out at the sides.

Not moving. Not moving at all.

I blinked hard, trying to force the image away.

But it didn't disappear. It remained, black against the dark gray of the bedspread.

A man's body. Mr. Crowell's body. Stretched—unmoving—on the bed.

"Ohh—!"

I had just enough time to cry out before two hands grabbed me from behind.

"*L*et *goooo!*" I managed to cry.

I twisted free. Spun around—and stared at Spencer.

"Sorry," he whispered. "I didn't mean to scare you. I thought you heard me coming. I—"

"Spencer—on the bed!" I choked out. "Mr. Crowell—he's . . . he's . . ."

Spencer moved quickly to the bed. He reached down with both hands—and lifted the body easily.

And held it up to me.

"Huh?" I gasped. It took me a few seconds to realize that I hadn't been staring at a body after all.

"Pajamas," Spencer murmured. He balled them up and tossed them back on the bedspread. "Crowell wears black pajamas."

"And he spreads them out on the bed?" I cried breathlessly. I felt like such a jerk. I grabbed Spencer's arm. I needed something to hold on to for a moment. Something solid.

I held on to his arm as he led the way back to the front room. "Where are Cassie and Jordan and Lenny?" I asked.

Spencer didn't answer. He moved to the bookshelf against the wall.

Headlights filled the front window, then rolled over the wall. I glimpsed Spencer's face glowing white in the stark light.

A loud crash from the back made me jump. Jordan and Cassie hurtled down the hall toward us.

"It's Mr. Crowell!" Jordan called shrilly. "He's back. His car is in the driveway!"

"We have to get out of here!" Cassie squealed. "Now!"

I started toward the doorway. Cassie and Jordan were already running down the back hall. I reached for Spencer's hand, but my fingers brushed against something hard and cold. I squinted at him in the darkness.

He was carrying Mr. Crowell's CD player!

"Spencer—no!" I gasped. "That wasn't the plan! We weren't going to steal—remember?"

A car door slammed outside. In a second, Mr. Crowell would burst in and find us.

We hurtled in the dark to the side window where we had entered.

"It—it's shut!" I cried.

I grabbed it with both hands. Pushed hard. It didn't budge.

The front door slammed shut.

"He's inside!" Cassie hissed.

Lenny and I both pushed the window frame with all our might.

But the window was stuck.

I heard Mr. Crowell's light footsteps in the hall.

And knew we were caught.

chapter
15

Was Crowell outside the room?

If we ran into the hallway, would we bump right into him?

We had no choice. We had to take the chance.

Our escape route to the side of the house had been blocked. We had to try the kitchen door.

"Let's go!" Spencer cried.

We stampeded after him.

I struggled to hear Mr. Crowell's footsteps. His voice. A cough. Anything.

But the only sounds I could hear were the pounding of my heart and the thud of our shoes on the hard floor as we made our way to the kitchen.

A moment later, we pushed our way out the door, into the night. The cold wind shocked my hot face. I gasped and forced myself to run deeper into the darkness.

Was that Mr. Crowell shouting behind us?

Or was it a dog howling at the moon?

I didn't stop to figure it out.

We ran through the dark, empty yards. We didn't slow down, even though we knew we were safe. We knew we had escaped.

As we crossed the street that led to Spencer's block, Lenny let out a cheer. It became the signal for us to celebrate, to whoop and shout and cry out our victory.

And still we ran.

Will I ever forget the sight of Spencer, his blond hair flying as he ran full speed, ran bringing his knees up high, almost strutting, ran with Mr. Crowell's CD player gripped tightly in both hands?

No. I don't think I'll ever forget that sight.

And I know I'll never forget his grin, his wild, spinning eyes, his crazy expression of excitement, of triumph.

Spencer . . . Spencer . . .

I was still thinking about him minutes later as I crept back into my house and up the stairs to my room. I closed the door behind me and started to get undressed in the dark.

"Diane?"

Mom's voice nearly made me jump out of my skin.

"Diane?" She knocked twice on the door. The door started to swing open.

I dove for my bed. Somehow I managed to slide— fully dressed—under the bedspread before she poked her head into the room.

"Diane? Is everything okay? I thought I heard something."

I yawned and pretended I'd been asleep. "Mom?" I choked out. "What's wrong?"

"I thought I heard someone walking around," she replied. In the darkness, I could see her peering around the room.

"I—I'm okay," I whispered. "Just . . . so sleepy."

"Sorry, dear." A few seconds later, the door closed again. I could hear her soft footsteps heading back to her room.

I waited a few seconds longer, my heart pounding. Then I climbed out of bed. A close call, I knew.

We'd had a *few* close calls tonight.

I changed into a long nightshirt. But I knew I was too wired to fall asleep. I carried my cordless phone to bed and punched in Cassie's number.

She answered after less than a ring. "It's me," I said.

"I can't sleep, either," Cassie offered before I could get in another word. "I'm totally crazed."

"It was kind of fun," I confessed. "I mean, it wasn't boring!"

We both laughed.

"Not trashing Crowell's house was a good idea," Cassie remarked. "But almost getting caught was a really bad idea!"

"And once again Spencer went too far," I groaned.

Cassie was silent for a moment. "Yeah. What's *with* that guy?" she asked finally. "It's like he always has to go one step further than we do. Like he always has to top us."

"Yeah. I know," I quickly agreed. "It's like one thrill isn't good enough for Spencer. He isn't satisfied unless he does something really dangerous."

"Weird," Cassie replied softly. "The whole thing about Spencer is so weird. He used to be so shy. We all used to think he was a joke. Now, even Lenny and Jordan think he's great."

"That's what kind of scares me," I confessed. "If they see Spencer steal a CD player, I hope they won't want to start stealing, too."

"Hey—Lenny should be happy," Cassie said. "He got his revenge on Mr. Crowell. That's all he cared about."

"I hope so," I replied.

Cassie and I chatted for a few minutes more. Then I realized I was starting to feel sleepy, so I said good night and hung up.

I was carrying the phone back to its base on my desk when it rang again. Startled, I raised it to my ear. "Cassie? What did you forget?" I said. Cassie can never talk just once. She always calls back at least once or twice.

"I saw what you did tonight," a whispered voice rasped, harsh and menacing in my ear.

"Huh? Cassie?" I gasped.

"I know about your Night Games, Diane."

Hey. This was *not* Cassie. "Bryan?" I cried. "Bryan—are you back again?"

"I know what you stole tonight. I know about your little revenge."

"Bryan—you're not scaring me!" I snapped through gritted teeth. "You might as well give up."

72

I realized I was squeezing the phone tightly. I carefully relaxed my grip.

I could hear heavy breathing now. Slow and steady.

"Bryan—is that you?" I demanded. "Is it?"

"You'll pay, Diane," came the raspy reply. *"You're going to pay for what you did."*

chapter

16

I turned off the light and huddled under the covers. I stared at the ceiling. At the walls.

At the phone.

I didn't sleep all night.

The next day I dragged around school like a zombie. But the bell for fourth period woke me with a start.

Fourth period. Mr. Crowell's class.

I walked toward the room. Wide awake with pure fear.

I thought of going to the nurse's office and pretending I felt sick. But I couldn't desert Jordan, Cassie, and Lenny.

I reached the room as the last bell rang. Everyone else had taken a seat. I clutched my books to my chest and quickly found my seat.

Mr. Crowell's tiny black eyes were fixed on me. Any

second I expected him to shout out my name. To accuse me, in front of everyone, of trashing his house. To accuse the four of us.

But he didn't say a word. Just stared at me coldly.

My hands trembled as I opened my notebook and looked up at the board. Mr. Crowell turned to the board and began furiously writing an algebra equation. The chalk made a scratchy sound that gave me chills.

I glanced over at Cassie. She chewed the top of her pen. Then she turned to me and, without making a sound, she mouthed the words, "Think he knows?"

I shrugged. Just then, Mr. Crowell spun around and stared at Cassie. "Give me the next step in this equation," he demanded.

Cassie shifted in her seat and cleared her throat.

"Well? We don't have all day," he snapped.

She mumbled some numbers and Crowell wrote them on the board.

"But I *nearly* caught you," he said to Cassie. "Didn't I?"

Cassie sat up even straighter. She blinked, but didn't answer.

Then Crowell stared at me again with his cold black eyes. I felt like an insect pinned to a dissection tray. My stomach clenched in a hard knot.

Finally, his gaze moved to Lenny.

Lenny stared right back at him. His arms crossed over his chest. His jaw thrust out. He didn't look the least bit nervous.

Only I knew he was really freaked. Lenny has a habit of crossing his legs and shaking his foot when he's nervous. His foot was shaking so fast that his desk vibrated.

Crowell moved in front of Lenny. A cruel grin twisted his lips. Then he asked Lenny for the next step in the equation.

Cassie and I glanced at each other.

Was Crowell baiting Lenny? Just to have more fun when he finally accused him of breaking into his house?

Lenny stared at the board a long time. Crowell came even closer. He stared down at Lenny with his crow eyes.

Finally, Lenny gave the right answer.

Crowell turned away.

What was Mr. Crowell thinking? I wondered.

Did he see us in his house? Did he know who stole his CD player? Did he know who moved his stuff around?

Maybe he was waiting until the end of class to corner us. What would he do? I could hardly keep still in my seat as I watched the big clock over the door. Each minute of class felt like an hour.

I sneaked secret looks at Jordan, Cassie, and Lenny. Crowell droned on, scratching out more equations.

Finally, the bell rang. I stood up slowly, weak in the knees. I gathered up my books. Everyone raced past me and rushed out the door.

Mr. Crowell's eyes met mine. I dropped my math book.

I always stuff my graded papers in between the pages. The papers flew out of the book and scattered across the floor.

I knelt down and frantically grabbed them. I didn't dare look up to see if Mr. Crowell was watching me. My hands shook as I picked up the papers. Then my science book fell and more papers hit the floor.

Crowell came over to help. "Diane, will you please stay for a few minutes?" he asked. "I want to talk to you."

My heart missed a beat. I couldn't say anything. Mr. Crowell handed me my old assignments, and I stuffed them into my book. We were all alone.

This was it. The moment I dreaded. He had seen me at his house. He was about to accuse me.

Mr. Crowell strolled back to his desk. He leaned casually against it.

"You're a good student, Diane."

I stared at him as if he had gone crazy. I rubbed a finger across my top lip to wipe away the sweat.

"Th-thanks, Mr. Crowell," I mumbled. When would he get to the point?

"I was wondering how you're doing on your midterm project," he continued. "Do you need any help?"

My midterm project?

I couldn't even remember what my project was about. Relief flooded through me.

"No, Mr. Crowell," I said, trying to keep my voice from quivering. "Everything is fine. I'm almost done."

He smiled. "Very good. You chose a difficult topic. I wanted to make sure you were clear on it. If you have any questions at all, please don't hesitate to ask. That's what I'm here for."

I could hardly believe it. Since when was Mr. Crowell so considerate? Was this his Christmas spirit or something? Was it possible that he hadn't recognized us?

"I'll make sure I see you if I have any problems," I promised. "Can I go now?"

He studied me for a moment and then nodded. "See you tomorrow."

I dashed out the door.

My friends waited for me at my locker. They looked worried as I hurried up to them.

Lenny reached out to hug me.

"Did Crowell keep you after?" Lenny asked. "I looked around and you weren't behind me."

"I dropped my book," I answered. "And you guys ran out of the classroom so quick, I was all alone with him."

"What did he say?" Cassie asked. She bit on her lower lip. "Does he know?"

"Did he say anything about last night?" Jordan demanded.

"Not a word." I shook my head. "He wanted to know how my midterm project is coming."

Cassie drew a deep breath. Jordan let out a nervous giggle.

"I think the Night Games have to stop," I announced.

"Why?" Lenny asked. "Crowell doesn't know who broke into his house. He would have come down on us if he did."

"Maybe he doesn't know now," I answered, "but I'm afraid he's going to find out."

"Diane is right," Cassie said. "He kept staring at us during the whole class. This isn't fun anymore. I want to stop, too."

"Just chill, you two," Jordan scoffed. "He doesn't have a clue."

"That's right," Lenny agreed. "Every kid in school hates him. It could have been anyone. He's so mean, it could have been his mother!"

78

Jordan chuckled. Even Cassie smiled.

I didn't think it was so funny.

These Night Games had started as harmless fun. Something different. Exciting. But now I didn't know where we were headed.

"Come on, Diane. Lighten up," Lenny said, squeezing my arm. Then he glanced at Jordan. I could tell they thought I was acting like a wimp.

But I didn't like what was happening. Shaking my head, I turned to my locker and yanked open the door.

"Someone called me last night after I got home," I told the others.

Lenny's smile disappeared. His eyes narrowed. "Who called you?" he demanded jealously.

"I don't know. But someone knows what we did at Mr. Crowell's. The person threatened me."

I'm not sure why I did it. But I turned my gaze toward Jordan.

He frowned. And then he blushed.

Weird. Jordan blushing? He *never* blushes.

He glanced away.

"Who would threaten you?" Lenny asked.

I shrugged. The voice had sounded so familiar. Yet, I couldn't figure out who it was.

Bryan came to mind. But I didn't mention him. I knew if I mentioned his name, Lenny would start a fight.

"This is serious, Diane," Lenny said. "If you even have a wild guess, you'd better tell."

"I know it's serious!" I cried. I twisted away from him. "That's why we've got to stop. It's just plain stupid to keep doing it. What if the caller phones the police?"

Lenny frowned. "Yeah, I guess you're right," he

admitted. "If someone is watching us, we have to stop."

"I think you're all getting bent out of shape over nothing," Jordan scoffed.

"Diane was threatened," Lenny replied in a tough voice. "I don't call that *nothing.*"

"I'm all for stopping," Cassie said eagerly.

"Well, we need to tell Spencer," I said.

Jordan rolled his eyes. "Great. He'll think we're all total wimps."

"Grow up, Jordan!" Cassie snapped. "Who cares what he thinks? We're the ones who have to face Crowell every day."

"Fine," Jordan replied. "Let's go to his house after school."

I met my friends in the parking lot after last period, and we walked over to Spencer's house together.

Lenny knocked on the front door and rang the bell. No answer.

"Doesn't look like he's home from school yet," Jordan said.

"He's probably hanging out with someone interesting over at St. Ann's," Jordan said.

"You mean someone like a girl?" Lenny scoffed. "Spencer? Give me a break!"

"Hey, it could happen," Cassie replied with a little smile. "Spencer is pretty cute now—not like he used to be."

Jordan chuckled. "Well, he's not fat anymore. But he's still weird looking."

"He is one ugly dude," Lenny agreed with a harsh laugh.

The two guys cracked up and Cassie made a face at them.

"I guess we can't talk to Spencer now," I said. "Let's just tell him tomorrow."

I had dinner at Cassie's house and stayed to study for our vocab test together. By the time I left, it was nearly nine o'clock.

The day had been cold and overcast. After dark, the mist from the river floated up into the town. A light snow fell.

I walk home from Cassie's house all the time. I usually don't mind being out at night all alone. But tonight, I felt nervous.

I found myself thinking about the phone call. The raspy voice. The knowledge that someone had followed me. Watched me when I didn't even realize it.

Was someone watching me now?

I glanced quickly over my shoulder. Out of the corner of my eye, I saw something—or someone— moving out of the shadows.

Then I realized that it was only a mailbox tilting in the wind.

Get a grip, Diane, I scolded myself. You're freaking out over a mailbox.

I took a deep breath and kept walking. Down two more blocks and left at the stop sign. I told myself I was acting stupid, but I couldn't shake off the feeling of being watched.

I sensed someone close behind me.

Hiding in the misty shadows.

I turned down my street. My house came into sight. A warm yellow light shone in the front windows.

I started past our neighbor's yard. Thick boxwood hedges lined the sidewalk. I remembered how I hid in them when I was a little kid. They were so thick, no one could find me.

As I walked past, a hand shot from the hedges and caught my wrist in a strong grip. Fingers dug hard into my skin.

I screamed. My books flew out of my arms as I twisted to loosen the grip.

The hand tightened, twisting my arm up behind my back.

I couldn't move. I opened my mouth to scream but a hand clamped down over my mouth.

"Diane, what's your problem?" the attacker cried. "It's only me!"

Bryan?

I took a gulp of air.

Only Bryan.

Finally the grip on my wrist relaxed. I yanked my arm away and spun to face him. Bryan ran a nervous hand through his thick, brown hair.

My fear slowly drained away. Replaced by anger. "Are you crazy?" I snapped.

"I want to talk," he answered. "Please."

"Were you following me?"

He glanced away, then back. "Yes," he murmured. "I saw you go over to Cassie's tonight. I came here to wait for you."

"First your phone calls and now this?" I asked. "What is your problem?"

He gazed at the ground. "Why won't you give me a chance? I waited out here in the snow all night just to see you."

"Well, I'm so sorry you had to hang around," I

replied nastily. I turned away from him. But he followed me.

"I won't leave until you talk to me," he insisted.

"Go get a life, Bryan," I snapped. "I don't want to go out with you. How many times do I have to say it?"

"We could try again," he pleaded. Bryan stepped toward me, and raised his hands. "Oh, come on, I won't hurt you," he said. "You must know that."

"Go away!" I insisted.

"You deserve a better guy than Lenny," he whined.

"And I suppose you're the one I need, huh?"

"You need someone to protect you," he insisted.

I stared at him in shock. "Protect me? From what?"

"Lenny is a hothead. He'll get you mixed up in something bad. I know what I'm talking about, Diane."

How much did he know? Had he been the one following us last night after all?

"You don't know anything, Bryan," I snapped. "Why don't you just leave me alone? I'm not getting back together with you. And I've had enough of your threatening phone calls."

A confused look crossed Bryan's face. He shook his head. "Huh? Threatening calls?" he asked.

"Stop lying!" I yelled. "You've been spying on me! You've been watching me and my friends! And you called me and threatened me!"

"What are you talking about?" he cried. "I only called you once. And I didn't threaten you, Diane. What are you so upset about?"

"Forget it, Bryan," I said. "Stay away from me." I turned to run.

But his strong hands closed on my arms and turned me roughly to face him. "I want to talk," he insisted in a menacing voice. "Why won't you just talk to me?"

My anger dissolved. Fear flooded through me.

His grip felt so strong. Like a vise.

I gasped and tried to pull away again.

He squeezed harder.

"Let go, Bryan," I begged. "You're hurting me. Let go. What are you *doing?*"

chapter

17

"*B*ryan, let go!" I cried.

The bright headlights of a passing car flashed on us. Bryan jumped, and his grip on my arms loosened. I jerked away from him. "Stay away from me and my friends," I said.

Bryan stared at me for a second. Then he turned and ran up the block.

I watched him disappear into the darkness. My heart pounded against my ribs. I took a few shaky steps and turned into my driveway.

I let myself in the side door and stepped into the kitchen. The house seemed very quiet. I found a note on the kitchen table from my parents. They were at a community fund-raiser for the evening.

Perfect, I thought. I have the house to myself!

After all that had happened in the last couple of days, I needed time alone to relax. I grabbed a diet soda and strolled into the den. I stretched out on the sofa and grabbed the TV remote.

But before I turned on the set, I heard a loud knock on the front door.

I froze. Bryan again? Couldn't he take a hint and give up?

Another knock. Louder. I stomped to the door. "What do you want?" I yelled.

"Diane, it's me. Open up," I heard Lenny call. I flung open the door. Lenny stared back at me. I could tell he was upset.

"I need to talk to you, Di," he said breathlessly.

I pulled him into the house. "What's wrong?" I asked.

He glanced around. "I didn't see your dad's car. Are your folks home?"

"No. They're at some dinner," I replied. "Come sit down. You look terrible."

He followed me silently into the den. We sat on the sofa. I touched his arm and felt him shaking. "What happened?" I asked in a low voice.

He leaned forward and rubbed his hands across his face. "Crowell called my parents and told them why I was kicked off the team."

"Oh, Lenny! Why?"

"My dad said he did it to help me learn responsibility," he answered. "Do you believe that?"

"Bad scene with your parents?" I asked.

"The worst," he admitted. "I'm in major trouble. My mom kept saying I couldn't get into college with my terrible grades."

"They're worried about you," I said gently.

Lenny nodded. "I know. I'm not angry at them. I

just wish Crowell had given me a chance to talk to
them first. Now they won't listen to anything I say.
They didn't even give me a chance to explain. That
jerk—" Lenny picked up a pillow from the couch and
pounded it with his fist. "I'm in trouble now. Big
time. All because of him."

I tried to come up with some comforting words. But
I didn't know what to say. I had seen Lenny upset
before about getting into trouble with his folks. But
never this bad.

Lenny sat back and studied me for a second. "I
need to tell you something, Diane," he whispered.
"Something that no one else knows."

"What?" I asked.

He stared down at the sofa pillow in his hands. He
set it aside. Then he spoke quickly. "I keep having
these daydreams. Horrible fantasies. I see myself
beating up Mr. Crowell. On the way over here, I
imagined that I ran him down with my car."

I swallowed hard.

That didn't sound like Lenny. Yes, he definitely had
a bad temper. But would he really beat up a teacher?
No way.

"Lenny, you have to try to talk to Mr. Crowell," I
told him. "Tomorrow. It will get worse if you don't.
We still have over half the school year left."

He scowled at me and didn't say anything.

"Maybe he'll be reasonable," I continued. "He's
not *that* bad."

For a moment, I thought Lenny would answer me.
But then the scowl returned and his gaze went blank. I
knew he hadn't heard a word I said. So I did the only
thing I could think of: I kissed him.

He didn't react at first.

Then his arms came up around my back. He pulled me close. Hugged me. Hugged me tight.

I felt him trembling. My heart ached to help him. But I couldn't do anything—except be the one who accepted him the way he was.

Lenny kissed me again. I felt him relax a little.

Then a loud sound filled the room.

Pounding at the front door.

I jumped at the noise. Lenny drew back. "Who could that be so late?" he asked fretfully.

I shook my head and pulled away. "I'll be right back." I padded to the door. "Who's there?" I called.

No reply.

Bryan, I thought.

"Who is it?" I repeated sharply.

Still no answer.

A surge of anger filled me. I was sick of being scared.

I pulled open the door.

chapter

18

Cassie stood on the front porch. Her usually neat hair stood out in all directions. Her eyes were wild.

"Oh, Diane!" she cried. "You're not going to believe this."

"What's wrong?" I asked, shutting the door behind her.

She dug into her purse and pulled out a piece of paper.

"Look what I found in my bag," she answered. Flipping the sheet of paper open, she read: "I know about your Night Games. You're going to be the loser." She raised her eyes to me. "I don't recognize the handwriting."

My heartbeat quickened. "Who is doing this to us?" I cried.

Lenny appeared at the front hall. "What's the matter, Cass? Are you okay?"

Cassie shook her head. "No. None of us is okay."

She shoved the note at him and stormed into the den. Cassie flopped onto the couch with an enormous sigh. I sat down next to her. But she didn't say anything more.

Lenny handed the note back to Cassie.

"It's Mr. Crowell," he said.

"Mr. Crowell?" Cassie repeated. "You think he's writing notes and phoning Diane in the middle of the night?"

"Who else could it be?" he answered.

Cassie glanced at me. "Diane, your boyfriend is cute. But he's crazy."

"Tell me about it," I replied. I smiled at Lenny, but he didn't smile back.

"It has to be Mr. Crowell," Lenny insisted. He paced back and forth in front of us. "That man is really twisted. There's no telling how far he'd go to torture us. That's how he gets his kicks. By making our lives miserable."

"He wouldn't go that far," Cassie argued. "You just think it's Crowell because you hate him."

"He's the only one who could have spotted us," Lenny insisted. "You saw how he glared at us in class, didn't you?"

"Yeah," Cassie answered. "But why would he slip a note into my purse? He could call the police and get us all into real trouble."

I shook my head at Lenny. "I don't think it was Mr. Crowell, either. He may not like us, but put a note into Cassie's bag? Come on!"

"Yeah," Cassie agreed. "Diane is right."

"I think it was Bryan," I announced.

90

"Bryan?" Lenny asked. He gazed at me curiously. "What does that creep have to do with this?"

I hesitated. I didn't want Lenny to get into another fight with Bryan.

"Diane," he urged impatiently, "what's going on?"

I decided to tell him. "Nothing is going on," I said firmly. "Bryan wants to go out again. He's been following me. He's acting really strange, too. I told him to go away and leave me alone."

"Well, if he tries to talk to you again," Lenny said, "tell me. I'll take care of it."

"No, Lenny—" I started.

"Don't worry," he assured me. "I won't hit him. With Mr. Crowell on my case, I can't afford to get into any more fights."

I sat beside Lenny. He slipped his arm around my shoulders.

"Well, we've pretty much run out of suspects," Lenny said matter-of-factly. "It has to be Bryan."

"Maybe not," Cassie said. "How about Spencer?"

Lenny and I both stared at her. "Why Spencer?" Lenny asked.

"Haven't you noticed?" Cassie replied. "He's so different now."

Lenny snorted. "And you thought I was nuts for suspecting Mr. Crowell! This whole thing was Spencer's idea. Why would he try to scare us?"

Cassie frowned. "I don't know. But I've been thinking—Spencer's sense of humor is so warped now. He really got a charge out of scaring that couple in the car. And he loved smashing up Mr. Crowell's Christmas decorations."

I remembered Spencer's wild laughter as we ran

down the street. "He liked stealing the CD player, too," I added.

"So he likes excitement," Lenny scoffed. "What's so bad about that?"

"The wrong kind of excitement," I pointed out.

"But Spencer loves to play the Night Games," Lenny argued. "It doesn't make any sense that he would try to stop them."

"No one said it had to make sense," I answered. "We haven't seen Spencer in a year. He could have gone through all kinds of changes during that time."

"He does seem really . . . different," I agreed. "Did you ever notice that—"

Someone knocked on the door.

I stopped talking and stared at my friends. Cassie licked her lips nervously.

More pounding. I took a deep breath. "Why does everyone come to *my* house?" I muttered. I strode to the front door.

"Who is it?" I called out.

"It's me," Spencer called back. "Open up."

I pulled open the door.

He stared at me frowning, biting his bottom lip. "I can't believe it, Diane!" he said finally. His voice trembled. He dug in the pocket of his jeans and pulled out a note. "Look at this."

I glanced at it—the same handwriting as on Cassie's note. "Cassie got one, too," I told him. "She and Lenny are already here. Come in."

He followed me to the den. He nodded to Lenny and Cassie.

"Spencer got a note, too," I said. "It looks just like Cassie's."

"I found it stuck under the windshield wiper of my car," Spencer reported.

"What does it say?" Lenny asked.

Spencer looked down at the note and read it aloud.

"Night Games can be dangerous," he read quietly. "Sometimes people die."

Last Winter

chapter
19

*B*y the time Spencer awoke, deep snow had drifted against the windows. He rolled out of bed and stumbled to the kitchen. He made a cup of hot chocolate, then went out onto the deck of the cabin.

Quiet out here.

Spencer drew a deep breath. He liked the snow. And the quiet it brought.

If only I had someone to share it with, he thought. Someone like Diane.

He glanced toward the window of her room. Maybe she would get up before the others. Maybe she would join him.

"Hey, Spence!" He turned to see Cassie, wearing neon-blue ski pants and a bright blue jacket.

Diane followed her out onto the deck. Her long, blond hair was woven in a braid. She yanked a blue knit cap low over her forehead and flashed Spencer a smile. His heart surged.

He remembered how it felt to kiss her. But then he thought of Lenny's punch.

Spencer touched his mouth. Still sore.

"We're going out to play in the snow," Diane said brightly. "Lenny and Jordan are getting ready now. Come with us, Spencer?"

"Let me grab my coat," he answered. He followed the girls through the cabin and outside.

Cassie turned a circle in the deep snow and fell backwards. She swished her arms up and down.

"What are you doing?" Spencer called.

"Making a snow angel, of course!" she cried.

Diane grabbed Spencer's hand and pulled him down into the snow. They sprawled there giggling and making angels until Lenny and Jordan showed up.

Spencer glanced up at them. The expression on Lenny's face frightened him. He hasn't forgiven me for kissing Diane, Spencer realized.

"Look at that, Len," Jordan said. "Spencer's moving in on our girlfriends."

"Hey—he's a lot more fun than you!" Cassie teased.

Lenny snorted in reply. "Then you can be on Spencer's side," he snapped.

"What do you mean?" Diane asked.

"A snowball war!" Lenny declared. "Jordan and me against you, Cassie, and Spencer."

Diane giggled. "Okay, you're on." She held out her hands for Lenny to help her up. Diane pulled away and kicked through the snow. "Come on, guys!" she yelled.

Laughing, Cassie ran after her. Spencer followed

slowly. He couldn't shake the feeling that Lenny had something nasty planned. More than just a snowball fight.

The girls started the battle. They launched a couple of snowballs at Lenny's head. He ducked.

Cassie squealed. Jordan pelted her, and she fell back into the snow.

Spencer saw Lenny glaring at him.

I hate that guy. I can't believe he came to my uncle's cabin when I didn't even invite him, Spencer thought bitterly.

Diane and Cassie tossed handfuls of snow. Spencer bent down and began packing his own snowballs— extra hard. Then he melted them with his hand to form a layer of ice.

He waited until Lenny turned away. Then he picked up an iceball and pitched it at Lenny with all his strength. It sped through the cold, clear air.

Spencer watched in horror as it whizzed past Lenny—and smacked Jordan on the side of the head.

Jordan uttered a cry and went down as if he had been hit with a hammer.

Before Jordan could get up, Spencer grabbed another iceball and hurled it at Lenny. Direct hit. It slammed Lenny in the mouth. He yelped and reached for his face.

Spencer smiled grimly. That's for punching me last night, he thought.

Spencer saw a thin trickle of blood at the corner of Lenny's mouth. Lenny wiped it with his glove. Drops of blood stained the white snow.

Lenny yanked Jordan to his feet and pointed at Spencer. Jordan rubbed his head.

Lenny and Jordan stalked angrily toward Spencer.

Spencer felt the bitter taste of fear rise up in his throat.

Diane stopped throwing snowballs. "What are you guys doing?" she cried.

"Spencer is using iceballs," Lenny growled.

Both girls stared at Spencer. "Why?" Diane demanded.

Spencer couldn't meet her eyes. He shrugged. "I didn't mean to. Maybe they froze."

Lenny and Jordan stopped on either side of Spencer. "Maybe they *froze?*" Lenny repeated. "Give it up! You made them hard as a rock."

Spencer felt his heart pounding. What was I thinking? he wondered. He was no match for Lenny—and definitely not for both Lenny and Jordan.

He tried to sound tough. But his voice shook anyway. "It's only a dumb snowball fight. Why don't you just chill, Lenny?"

Lenny snorted. "Why don't *you?*"

He jumped forward. Jordan moved at the same time. They shoved him headfirst into a deep snowdrift.

"Let's bury him!" Jordan yelled.

"Excellent!" Lenny cried, laughing.

Get away! instructed a voice in Spencer's head. Crawl away from them!

He struggled to move. Tried to wipe the snow from his eyes.

But Lenny held his arms. Then sat on his legs.

Spencer yanked one arm loose. But snow filled his eyes and his mouth.

White all around now. Frozen white.

Which way? Spencer thought frantically. Which direction is up? He clawed blindly at the snow.

But it felt so heavy on his arms. Heavy on his back.

He felt them pile more snow on top of him. Felt its weight crush him down. Down. Even deeper into the white.

He gasped for air. But with every effort at breathing, he took in a mouthful of snow.

Drowning, he thought. I'm drowning in snow.

From far away he heard Diane and Cassie laughing.

Lenny and Jordan chanted, "Bury him! Bury him!"

"Please stop," Spencer pleaded. But the snow filled his mouth. His tongue felt frozen. Numb. He gagged, his mouth stuffed with icy snow.

"Lenny!" Spencer heard Diane's voice. "Stop. He'll freeze!"

Lenny's laughter sounded miles away. "It's just a joke!"

Just a joke. The words echoed in Spencer's head. *A joke.*

The icy cold penetrated his clothes and boots. He had no feeling in his hands. His arms. His feet and legs.

So dark inside the snowdrift. So quiet.

The weight of the snow pressed down. Crushing him.

Paralyzing him.

Voices came from a long way off. Laughing. Chanting.

"Bury him! Bury him!"

Alive.

Spencer pushed against the packed snow. Pushed against the frozen walls. Pushed with everything he had.

His muscles strained.

He remained packed in the snow.

Frozen.

Panic filled him. What could he do? How could he tell them he was freezing?

Calm down, he told himself. Stay calm.

Diane would get him out. She wouldn't let Lenny hurt him.

Voices. Muffled words. Spencer tried to concentrate on the sounds. They seemed so far away.

Pain shot up his right leg. He fought to move.

Tired. Too tired to try again.

Time passed. How long? He wasn't sure.

He heard Lenny's voice. Louder than before. "Race you home, Spencer!" Lenny called.

"We can't leave him here." Diane's voice. "He'll freeze."

"He's okay," Jordan said. "He's just angry . . . wants us to think he can't get out."

Spencer strained to hear the voices. I can't move! he wanted to scream. Help me! Somebody, please!

I can't get out!

"Let's head back to Shadyside." Lenny's voice again.

"We can't leave Spencer." Diane arguing with him.

"He has a car. He can get back on his own." Whose voice was that? He felt confused. Who was talking?

The voices faded away.

Silence.

Spencer wondered if he had fallen asleep. He felt so tired now. So sleepy.

He heard a car start.

The sound made Spencer alert.

Jordan's Jeep! They started up the Jeep!

Terror warmed Spencer. He pushed against the snow with everything he had. He opened his mouth to scream, but it filled with more snow. The only thing that could scream now were his thoughts.

They couldn't drive away! They couldn't leave him here. Buried in the snow.

Buried alive.

Come back, he wailed silently.

I can't move. I can't breathe.

I'm so cold.

Diane, please. You're not going to leave me here to die.

You're not going to leave me.

Are you?

This Winter

chapter
20

"Diane!" I heard Cassie calling me from across the cafeteria. "Over here!"

Cassie always gets to the lunchroom before me on Thursdays. She saves our usual table.

I spotted her and carried my tray over. Lenny and Jordan sat across from her. I took the empty chair next to Cassie.

"I don't know why I bothered buying food," I told them. "I'm too nervous to eat."

Lenny grabbed half of my turkey sandwich and began wolfing it down.

"I know what you mean," Cassie said. "I couldn't sleep last night. I was too wired about Spencer's note."

"It gave me the creeps," Jordan said. "I mean, it sounded like someone wants to kill us."

"It sounds like some kind of sick joke to me," Lenny said.

"I don't get it," Cassie said fretfully.

"We should have told Spencer last night that we weren't going to play any more Night Games," I told them. "Isn't that what we agreed to do?"

We were all set to tell Spencer that it was over. Why hadn't we said anything last night when he came to my house with the note?

"What are we doing that's so bad?" Jordan asked with a shrug. "We're only playing games."

"Spencer stole something!" Cassie cried. "We could all get in trouble for that. And now someone is threatening us!"

Jordan nodded solemnly. "I guess you're right," he admitted. "Obviously someone knows about us. I wish we could figure out who it is."

I thought of all the suspects again. First Bryan. Did he send the threatening notes and make the telephone calls?

Who else could it be?

Mr. Crowell? No one but Lenny would believe that.

Cassie had suspected Spencer.

Then he turned up with that note.

Bryan was the only one it could be.

But why? Why would he try to frighten us?

And what would he do next?

Lenny agreed to talk to Mr. Crowell if I promised to wait outside the classroom while he did it.

Classes had ended for the day. I walked Lenny to Mr. Crowell's room and I stood in the quiet hall, near the classroom door. Lenny wore nice, clean khakis and a dark blue pullover sweater. He even combed his hair. I knew he wanted to impress Mr. Crowell.

It didn't work.

I planned to eavesdrop on the conversation. But I didn't have to, because Lenny and Mr. Crowell started screaming at each other loud enough for the whole school to hear.

I glanced around nervously. Should I go in and stop them? What if Lenny lost control and punched him? He would be expelled from school.

I reached for the doorknob. Before I touched it, the door swung open and slammed against the wall. Lenny shoved past me and stalked down the hall.

He didn't look at me.

I sprinted after him and finally caught up with him near the gym. Lenny stopped short in front of the open doors. I heard the sounds of the basketball team practicing inside.

Uh-oh, I thought, Lenny's really going to lose it now.

His hands balled into fists. His face shone bright red with fury.

"Are you all right?" I asked.

"You were wrong, Diane," he said through gritted teeth.

"What happened with Mr. Crowell?" I demanded.

"He said I was wasting his time. He said I would never change." Lenny's voice shook with rage. "He called me a loser."

"So you lost it? You blew up at him?"

Lenny's head whipped around. He glared at me. "What was I supposed to do?" he shouted. "Just stand there and let him call me names?"

Jordan ran off the basketball court and came to the doors. He caught Lenny's eye and they nodded at each other.

I felt a chill sweep through my body. I had never seen Jordan and Lenny so grim. So determined. So angry.

"What will you do?" I whispered. I gripped his hand.

He squeezed my fingers so hard it hurt.

"One more Night Game, Diane," Lenny said through clenched teeth. "One more visit to Mr. Crowell's house."

chapter

21

We met behind Spencer's house at midnight. The temperature had dropped during the afternoon, and the night air froze my breath into smoky clouds.

I shivered in my leather jacket. Lenny didn't wear a coat. I don't think he even noticed the cold.

Jordan and Cassie clung to each other. It was too cold for them to fight. Nobody spoke.

We waited for half an hour before Spencer finally climbed out of his house. He didn't apologize for being late. Instead he led us off into the night without a word. His expression matched Lenny's.

Solemn. Determined.

The empty streets echoed our footsteps. I looked at the darkened houses. I imagined people asleep inside. I wished that I was home in my own bed. Not out in the freezing cold, creeping through the shadows.

I watched Spencer as he walked in front of us. He wore all black again. His graceful movements made me think of a panther. A night stalker.

When did he change so much?

We reached Mr. Crowell's house. It looked empty. No Christmas lights blazing. No car in the driveway.

Lenny crept up to the side window we had used before. I grabbed his arm.

"What if he's waiting for us in there?" I whispered. Lenny jerked his arm away. I turned to Spencer. "What if he called the police and they're waiting for us? This is stupid!"

"Come on, Diane," Spencer urged. "You've come this far. It's only a joke."

"I don't care if he's home or not," Lenny snarled. "Let's go in. I hope he *is* home!"

Lenny pushed past me to get at the window. I couldn't move. My legs suddenly felt trembly and weak.

The mood tonight frightened me. None of the other Night Games had started this way.

With so much anger.

"Are you coming or not?" Lenny demanded.

Cassie sighed and clung to Jordan. Jordan nodded. I slowly followed him inside. I was so afraid, I expected Mr. Crowell to jump out at me at any second.

I took a single step into the dark room.

A loud crash made me scream.

My foot had tangled in an electric cord. I had knocked a lamp to the floor.

My friends snickered at me. I picked up the lamp and put it back. My hands shook as I patted the bent lamp shade back into shape.

The house was totally dark.

Cassie linked her arm through mine. I felt her trembling.

The guys fanned out into the room. Lenny stood directly in front of me.

The moon came from behind a cloud and washed eerie, white light through a window. It glinted off the metal in Lenny's hand.

A gun?

No! Not Lenny. Not a gun.

"Lenny!" I cried. "Are you crazy? What are you going to do with that?"

chapter

22

"*L*enny, please!" Cassie cried. She clung tightly to my hand. "Somebody is going to get hurt."

I couldn't speak. I could only stare at the glinting metal in Lenny's hand.

Lenny slowly raised his hand. He pointed. The dim light glistened on the gun.

I took a step backward. Time seemed to stop.

"Put it away," Cassie whispered.

"Just chill, you two," Lenny said. "Nobody is going to get hurt."

He swung his hand up.

"Get it away," Cassie insisted. She squeezed her eyes shut and clung to me.

I forced myself to look. At the spray-paint can.

Spray-paint can?

Relief rushed through me. I sighed. "Cassie, it's just spray paint," I said.

114

She opened her eyes and began laughing.

"What are you going to do with that?" I whispered.

Lenny smiled. "I thought I'd do a little redecorating."

"Lenny, don't!" I pleaded. "This is getting way out of control."

"Crowell deserves it," Lenny replied quietly.

He shook the paint can. The loud rattling echoed in the silent room.

"Lenny, no," I whispered. I tugged on his arm, but he shook me off.

He shook the can again. Took a step toward the wall.

My stomach tightened. My legs grew rubbery. But I stood and watched Lenny.

He walked up to the bookshelf and began spraying the paint in a thick zigzag all over the books. He whipped his arm around, changing from zigzags to big circles. Then spirals.

He laughed out loud. "Hey, this is fun! Want to try?"

"No way," I yelled back.

I couldn't take it anymore. I suddenly felt sorry for Mr. Crowell. This had gone too far.

I ran out of the room. Out into the dark hallway.

"Cassie?" I whispered. "Where are you?"

"Here!" she called. I stumbled forward in the darkness until I found her.

"We have to get out of here!" I cried. "This is horrible. I don't want to be a part of this!"

"Where are the guys?" Cassie asked.

"What do you mean?" I began. "They're right . . ." My voice trailed off as I realized that I couldn't hear Lenny's spray can anymore. I started to panic.

"Where are they?" I cried. "I don't hear them."

Cassie grabbed my hand and we inched along the wall. We slowly turned into the short hallway.

It seemed even darker here.

Suddenly I heard excited whispers. Cassie heard them, too. Her nails dug into my arm.

I took a step forward. Cassie walked so close behind me that she stomped on my heel. "Sorry," she whispered.

I followed the sound of the voices. It was so dark that I walked with my hands out in front of me to keep from bumping into things. The floorboards squeaked with each step.

Cassie clung to the back of my jacket.

I felt rough fabric. Wool. I moved my hand closer. A coat maybe.

A coat.

The coat moved. I screamed and stumbled back, as someone pulled the coat over my head.

I stumbled over Cassie. I heard her scream.

I pulled the heavy coat off my face—and grabbed at my attacker.

No one. An empty coat.

Attacked by a coat tree! I had walked into it in the dark.

I sat up, my heart pounding.

Cassie stood up and then helped me. I gasped for air. "I thought someone—"

"Me too," Cassie choked out. "The coat fell and—"

"Let's just find the guys and get out of here," I said.

She nodded. "Lead the way."

We started down the hallway again. Slow steps. My hands out straight. Feeling in the darkness.

I heard a gasp. Lenny's voice. My fingers met a dead end. The bedroom door—closed. I pushed it open. It made a loud squeaking sound.

Cassie let go of my jacket and disappeared into the dark room. I stood just inside the door. I squinted into the darkness.

The light flashed on. Cassie had found the wall switch.

I blinked against the bright light. I saw Spencer and Jordan. They stood close to each other. Staring down at something on the floor.

I followed their gaze.

Mr. Crowell!

Sprawled on the floor on his back. Legs out straight. Arms hanging stiffly at his sides. Fists clenched.

His cold, black eyes stared blankly up at the ceiling's glaring light.

He didn't blink.

Spencer leaned over him. Then he looked up at me. "He's dead," Spencer whispered.

chapter

23

My stomach lurched. I started to gag.

I covered my mouth with my hands.

I couldn't turn my eyes away from the figure sprawled so stiffly on the floor.

Mr. Crowell's body.

Cassie sank to her knees. She covered her face with her hands and began to moan.

I slowly walked over to Mr. Crowell. Any second he would come alive, I knew it. He would sit up and yell at us. Tell us it was a joke.

No. He remained perfectly still.

Frozen.

Spencer and Jordan stared at me, their faces chalk white.

I knelt down beside Mr. Crowell and forced myself to look at his face.

His skin shone with a sickly gray color. Brown circles under his eyes.

His thin lips were pulled tight, frozen in a grimace of pain.

His glasses lay on the carpet near his head. Shattered glass hung from the twisted frames. Both lenses were smashed.

My eyes wandered back to his body. A gnarled hand was flung out like a claw.

He must have been clawing for his glasses before he died. To see the terror he faced? To see his killer?

I reached out to touch his hand, but stopped.

The floorboards creaked and we all jumped. I turned to see Lenny walk into the room, grinning. He took one look at my face and stopped short. His jaw dropped in shock.

"What happened?" he asked.

No one answered.

I glanced back down at Mr. Crowell. Then nausea hit me again. I stumbled to my feet and gripped my stomach. I dove across the room, trying to stop the retching.

Who could have done this? Who hated Mr. Crowell enough to kill him?

Cassie hurried over and put her arm around me.

Jordan's voice broke the silence. "Don't touch anything," he ordered.

"How can he be dead?" I murmured.

"Who knows?" Jordan snapped. He stared at Lenny. "We didn't kill him. We have to get out of here. If the police find out we broke in . . ."

Lenny nodded grimly.

I couldn't make my mind work. Was Jordan right?

119

Was the teacher dead when we arrived? My thoughts ran wild.

Lenny.

Lenny hated Mr. Crowell so much.

Lenny had fantasies of killing him.

I stared at Lenny in horror. Lenny wasn't here when the rest of us found the body. Where was he?

No. Lenny couldn't kill Mr. Crowell. Lenny couldn't kill anyone, I told myself.

Spencer placed his hand on my shoulder. I jumped. "Come on, Diane," he said quietly. "We have to get out of here."

I couldn't move. Spencer knelt in front of me and gazed into my eyes. "Was it Lenny?" I whispered. "Did Lenny go too far?"

Spencer just stared at me.

"We have to leave," he said finally. He stood and pulled me up, then pushed me toward the bedroom door. The others already crept toward the side window.

Lenny stopped short.

"What's wrong?" Jordan asked.

"What do you think?" Lenny wailed. "I spray-painted the walls! The police will see it!"

Jordan grabbed Lenny's arm. "You didn't sign your name. Did you?"

Lenny shook his head. "No. But—"

"The police won't have a clue," Jordan told him. "Hurry up! Let's go!"

Lenny didn't budge.

"The spray can," he murmured. "Where's the can?" He began to search around frantically. "I can't leave without the can! It has my fingerprints on it!" His voice rose. "Where *is* it?" he cried.

"Where did you leave it?" I asked.

Lenny shook his head. "I tossed it somewhere. I wasn't thinking, I just threw it down! It could be anywhere!"

"We have to get *out* of here!" Cassie warned.

Jordan was pulling pillows off the couch, searching for the paint can.

I grabbed Lenny by the arms.

"Calm down and try to think," I urged. "Where were you when you stopped spraying the paint?"

Lenny groaned softly. He rubbed his hand across his forehead. "I don't know," he whispered. "I can't think straight."

"We have to go," Cassie repeated. "We have to get out of here—now!"

"Be quiet!" Jordan snapped.

"Get *down!*" Spencer cried.

I threw myself onto the hardwood floor just as the headlights of a car rolled across the wall behind me.

"The police!" Cassie gasped.

I pressed my hand over my mouth to keep from groaning out loud.

It was all over. Our lives were ruined.

We were caught!

chapter

24

I pressed myself against the floor; Spencer ducked beside me. He squinted up at the lights moving across the wall.

I heard Cassie's shallow breaths muffled against Jordan's shirt as he held her.

The headlights inched over the wall.

Someone was pulling into Mr. Crowell's driveway.

Lenny began crawling to the window. He raised himself on his knees and peered outside.

"It's not the police!" he whispered. "It's someone pulling into the driveway next door."

I felt so relieved! I wanted to shout for joy. But we all kept still while the people climbed out of the car and went inside. We heard car doors slamming. Finally Lenny whispered that they had gone inside.

"We have to be more careful than ever," Spencer warned. "Those people could look across the driveway and see us."

We started searching again for the can. Spencer wouldn't let us turn on any lights because of the neighbors. We hunted in the dark. Feeling around on the floor. The window ledges. Under furniture.

Nothing.

I stumbled into Cassie in the dark. She backed into a coffee table and sent a tiny glass Christmas tree crashing to the floor. It shattered into a thousand pieces.

"What are we going to do?" she wailed.

"Calm down!" I whispered. "As soon as we find the paint can, we can leave."

"Forget it! We have to leave without the can!" Spencer cried. "We can't stay here any longer!"

He pushed Cassie toward the window with one hand and yanked me along with the other.

His grip was so strong. "Spencer!" I squealed. "You're hurting me!"

"Sorry, Diane," Spencer replied breathlessly. "I didn't mean to hurt you."

"Will you two shut up and help me find the can?" Lenny barked. "I *can't* leave without it."

"Here it is!" Jordan shouted. "I found it."

We all turned to see him swoop down and reach under the Christmas tree. He stood up, waving the spray-paint can.

"Come on!" he ordered. "Let's move!"

We tumbled through the open window and sprinted

through Mr. Crowell's backyard. I climbed over the fence so quickly that I stumbled and scraped my hand. Before I even felt the pain, I was running again.

In the distance, a siren sounded. I stopped for a second. Fear gripped me, but Cassie pushed me ahead.

I started running again, but my legs felt like lead. I couldn't make them move any faster. I tried to push myself. I felt a burning pain in my side. It hurt more with each breath.

A couple of blocks later, Jordan tried to jump a fence and fell flat on his face. Lenny and Spencer never missed a step. They yanked him back onto his feet and charged off.

My leg muscles burned. My lungs felt as if they might burst. The wind brought tears to my eyes.

Fear drove me on.

Finally we reached my house. I whispered good night—and started to sneak into the house.

I heard the squeal of brakes from around the corner. I ducked down into the bushes as a car roared by.

Was it the police rushing to Mr. Crowell's house? Did one of the neighbors see us climb out of his window?

I peered between the bushes, trying to see the car. My breath caught in surprise. Not the police. A blue Toyota.

Bryan owned a blue Toyota.

I squinted hard, but I couldn't get a good look at the driver. Still, I knew Bryan's car. I had been in it enough to remember what it looked like. Even in the dark.

What was Bryan doing out so late at night? Spying on us? So he could blackmail us with more phone calls and threatening notes?

I pushed the questions from my mind. Feeling exhausted, I sneaked into my house and crept up to my room.

The warmth of my bedroom made me realize how cold I felt. My hands seemed like two chunks of ice. My fingertips stung. I tried to move my toes. But I had no feeling in my feet.

I sat down on my bed, still struggling to catch my breath. I wrapped myself in the thick down quilt.

I should never have gone with Lenny tonight, I told myself. We should have stopped before the Night Games got totally out of control.

Before Mr. Crowell was murdered.

I undressed quickly and pulled on a big T-shirt to sleep in. I tossed and turned all night. For hours I stared at the dark books lining the shelves above my desk. I kept picturing Lenny as he painted Mr. Crowell's books. I kept hearing Lenny's excited laughter.

I glanced at the alarm clock. Four o'clock in the morning. And the questions never ended.

What if someone saw us at Mr. Crowell's house? Would we be accused of killing him? Someone knew about our Night Games. That person could tell the police. The police would never believe we didn't kill the teacher.

The phone rang at seven o'clock. I rolled over and grabbed it.

"Did you hear the radio?" Cassie cried, without saying hello. "They found him."

I almost dropped the phone. I swallowed hard. "Found Mr. Crowell?" I choked out.

"Didn't you hear the news?" Cassie cried.

chapter

25

"*T*ell me," I demanded. "What did they say?"

"Mr. Crowell's housekeeper found him this morning," Cassie reported. "The police said he died of a heart attack."

I leaned back against my pillows and gasped with relief. "Huh? He had a bad heart!" I cried. "This means we're safe. They don't think someone killed him."

"Wrong. They do," Cassie replied.

A wave of dread quickly washed over me again.

"Lenny was such a jerk for spray-painting the walls," Cassie continued. "The police think an intruder broke in and scared Mr. Crowell to death."

I gasped.

"We're all in so much trouble!" Cassie wailed. "And all because of Lenny."

"Do you think it's true?" I asked.

"What?"

"That we scared Mr. Crowell and made him have a heart attack?"

She didn't reply.

"Cassie?"

"I don't know, Diane. I really don't."

Neither of us spoke.

"They're having an assembly today to honor Mr. Crowell," Cassie told me.

The idea of listening to speeches about Mr. Crowell all afternoon made my stomach queasy. I took a deep breath, hoping the nausea would go away. It didn't.

"Cassie," I murmured. "I won't be in school today."

I hung up and rushed for the bathroom.

"Diane—you look awful!" Mom cried when I finally made my way downstairs. "Do you have the flu?"

I wish! I told myself.

The flu would be gone in a couple of days. But my real troubles will hang around a lot longer.

Mom made me go to bed. I buried myself under the covers. As if the blankets would shield me from the awful truth.

None of my friends phoned me all day or evening. I think each one of us was in shock. Besides, there was nothing to talk about. Mr. Crowell was dead, and we might be responsible.

Still, it made me nervous that nobody called.

My parents went out as soon as Dad came home from work. They had tickets to a play downtown.

Mom felt bad leaving me, but I was happy. I needed to be alone.

I sat on the couch in the den, wrapped in a blanket. Dad rented a videotape for me. Anything to take my mind off Mr. Crowell!

The opening credits had just flashed by when someone knocked on the door.

I jumped at the sound. I won't answer, I decided.

But the knocking continued. Somebody pounded on the front door as if he or she wanted to break it down.

I clutched the blanket around me with icy fingers and slowly walked to the door.

As I reached it, the pounding stopped. I ran into the living room and peered out a window that faced the porch.

No one on the front porch.

I ran back to the door and opened it a crack. I looked around carefully. Just to make sure.

Not a soul in sight.

Frowning, I stepped outside. No one in the front yard.

I looked out at the street. I didn't see any parked cars, either.

I pulled the blanket up around me and turned back to the door.

Then I saw it.

A rolled-up sheet of paper propped against the porch railing.

With trembling fingers, I picked up the paper and carried it inside. I slammed the door shut and flipped all the locks.

I slowly unrolled the paper. The sheet was long.

Like a banner. As I carefully spread it out, my pulse sped up to double time.

Words spray-painted in red letters.

Terrifying words.

YOU DIE NEXT.

The words blurred in front of my eyes.

The letters were thick. Drippy. Like drops of blood on snow.

I rolled up the paper and stumbled to the phone. First I called Cassie. Then Lenny.

Cassie's mother told me Cassie was on her way to my house. Lenny's brother said the same thing.

When I hung up the phone, they were both on the front porch.

They both held rolled-up notes—just like mine.

Cassie unrolled her paper on my kitchen table. The same threats. The same spray paint. And the same handwriting.

"Do you recognize the writing?" Lenny asked. We didn't.

Lenny slammed his fist into the wall. "Who is doing this?" he cried.

131

"You tell us," Cassie answered nastily. "You don't still think it's Mr. Crowell, do you?"

He ignored her sarcastic remark. "Do you have any idea, Diane?" he asked.

"When I got home last night, I'm positive I saw Bryan drive by," I told him.

Lenny and Cassie stared at me without saying anything.

I continued. "Bryan drives a blue Toyota. It was his car. I'm sure of it. He could have been spying on us."

"But why would he send us these notes?" Cassie demanded. "What would he hope to gain?"

Lenny sighed. "Maybe he's just twisted."

"We need to find out if Jordan got one of these, too," I said. I glanced at Cassie. "Do you know where he is?"

She shook her head. "I called him when I got my note. But his mom said he was over at a friend's house, working on a science project. I don't know who."

"Let's go look for him," I suggested, rolling up my banner.

Lenny had his mother's car with him. We piled in and drove into town. We cruised up and down Division Street twice. Then we stopped at the mall and searched there. Finally we spotted Jordan's Jeep parked outside The Corner, a hangout near school.

"It's about time," Lenny muttered, pulling open the door to the restaurant.

I stopped short. I expected to see Jordan. I never expected him to be sitting with Bryan.

They shared the same booth. And the same plate of greasy fries. Jordan leaned across the table, deep in conversation with Bryan. Talking in low voices. They didn't even notice that we stood in the doorway.

My mind reeled.

Jordan and Bryan had never been good friends. Why would they hang out together now? What did they have to say to each other?

Whoa. Wait, I thought. Does Bryan know about our Night Games because Jordan told him? What were they planning?

Why would Jordan do this to us?

I stalked over to their table. "What are you doing with Bryan?" I demanded.

Jordan jumped. They both blinked at me in surprise.

"What's your problem, Diane?" Jordan snapped. "We're lab partners in chemistry."

"Aren't we allowed to discuss our project?" Bryan snapped. "Or do you want me to stay away from all your *friends,* too?"

"You *are* acting weird, Diane," Jordan put in. "Why are you so upset?"

Huh? We were all in huge trouble because of the Night Games—and Jordan couldn't guess why I was upset?

"You found the spray-paint can last night," I told Jordan.

"So?" he answered. "What about it?"

I pulled the rolled-up note from my pocket and slammed it onto the table. I spread it out so both of them could see the threatening message.

"Today we all got these horrible, spray-painted notes," I explained. "You sent them. Didn't you?"

Jordan snorted. He casually sipped his soda.

"Well?" I practically shouted. "Did you? Did you send these threats?"

A few kids in the next booth turned to stare at us.

Jordan's gaze leapt from me to Cassie to Lenny, and then back to me.

"All right, Diane," he said. "You guessed it. It *was* me. I sent the notes."

chapter
27

Jordan scowled. "I painted the notes," he admitted. "And I strangled Mr. Crowell with my bare hands, too. I'm also the Easter Bunny."

Bryan chuckled.

Jordan leaned toward me. "Diane, I thought we were friends," he said angrily. "How could you accuse me?"

"The spray-paint can," I replied. "The notes are all spray-painted, and you had the can."

Jordan's eyes blazed. "I don't have the dumb can, Diane. Spencer grabbed it away from me before we ran home."

My mouth dropped open.

"Are you telling us the truth?" Lenny asked.

Jordan frowned at Lenny. "So now *you* think I'm a liar, too?" He shook his head. "Some bunch of friends."

I drew a deep breath. Jordan was right. We should all trust one another. We had been friends for years.

"I guess we jumped to conclusions," I apologized. "I mean, *I* jumped to conclusions. I'm scared. But I didn't mean to blame you."

Jordan shrugged. "No big deal, Diane. It's a weird time for all of us."

"For sure," Lenny agreed. "Sorry, Jordan. I just sort of lost it for a second."

"But what *about* Spencer?" Cassie asked. "If he took the spray can, do you think he wrote the notes?"

Jordan shook his head. "Maybe it's a coincidence."

"Maybe it's a joke," Lenny put in.

"Great joke," Cassie sighed.

"Let's go find Spencer," I suggested. "We can all figure this out together."

Jordan nodded and stood up. He turned to Bryan. "Do you want to come?" he asked.

Bryan didn't even glance at me. He held his hands up and shook his head. "Leave me out of it," he announced. "I don't want anything to do with your games. I'm not getting dragged into this."

He got up and walked out without saying good-bye.

Cassie turned to me. "Guess he doesn't want you back that much!" she joked.

Cassie climbed into Jordan's Jeep, and Lenny and I followed them to Spencer's house.

"I never meant for Mr. Crowell to die, Diane," Lenny said, keeping his eyes straight ahead on the road. "I want you to know that."

I sighed. "I know. I wish we had never started playing these Night Games."

136

We pulled up and parked behind the Jeep. We all got out and stood on the sidewalk.

Spencer's house looked deserted. No lights anywhere. No car in the driveway. A loose window shutter creaked and groaned as it rocked back and forth on its hinges.

The sound sent shivers down my spine.

"This place could use some work," I muttered. "What a wreck."

We trudged through the leaves to the front door. Lenny rapped hard. We waited for a few seconds. No answer.

"Where *is* he?" I said, frustrated. "We all need to talk about this!"

I pulled away from Lenny. I walked to the front window and pressed my face against the glass. I peered inside, but saw nothing but darkness. Then the room slowly came into focus.

"Oh noooo!" I let out a horrified wail.

"Diane—what's wrong?" Cassie called from the front stoop.

I didn't answer her. I slid open the window and climbed through. The others piled in behind me.

It felt like a freezer inside. No heat.

The living room was totally empty.

No couch. No chairs. No furniture at all.

Spencer lay sprawled facedown on the wooden floor in the center of the room. His head twisted to one side.

He didn't move.

Cassie screamed. Jordan gasped and pulled back. Lenny swore under his breath.

"Spencer?" I cried. "Spencer? Spencer?" I ran to him and dropped to my knees.

I picked up his hand.

It felt spongy and cold.

Lifeless.

"He's dead," I whispered. "Spencer is dead."

chapter

28

"He—he's dead," I repeated, the words hanging in the cold, bare room.

The two boys huddled together, shock frozen on their faces.

Cassie crouched in the corner.

I dropped Spencer's hand and stood up. The room seemed to spin around me.

"I don't believe this!" Cassie wailed. "First Mr. Crowell. Now Spencer. Which one of us will be next? How did we get ourselves into this?" she sobbed.

Jordan hugged her tightly, trying to calm her down.

"What should we do?" I asked Lenny. "Call the police?"

He shook his head. "If we call them, we'll have to tell them everything—about the Night Games and Mr. Crowell. We'll be charged with murder. And no one will believe we didn't do it."

"Well, what then?" I replied. "Do we run away and pretend we don't know anything?"

Lenny shrugged. "Whoever killed Spencer is coming for us next," he said. "Maybe we *should* run away."

I turned away from him, struggling to think straight. My gaze fell on Spencer's body.

How long had he been lying here in this dark, empty place?

"Try the light switch," I told Lenny.

He flipped the switch. Nothing.

Lenny opened the bedroom door and peered into the shadows beyond. He disappeared down the hallway, his footsteps growing softer until I couldn't hear them.

"Where do you think Spencer's parents are?" Jordan asked.

"I don't know," I answered. "I guess they're not home."

Lenny burst through the door, his eyes wide. "Not home?" he repeated. "I don't think they're even in the same state!"

"What?" I cried.

Lenny jabbed a thumb toward the hall. "This whole house is empty. No furniture. No electricity. Nothing."

"It's like a freezer in here," Jordan added. "How did Spencer stand it?"

Cassie coughed again. "I told you Spencer changed," she reminded us. "Living in an abandoned house only proves it. Do you think we should try to find his parents?"

I turned back to Spencer.

"How did he die?" I asked.

"I don't know," Lenny replied. "It doesn't look like he was in a fight or anything."

"Then what happened?" I wondered.

"Does it matter?" Cassie wailed. "He's dead! We have to do something."

"M-maybe he's only unconscious," Jordan stammered. "We didn't check for a pulse or anything."

"Don't be ridiculous," I snapped. "Of course he's dead."

"You're right, Diane," whispered a raspy voice.

"Huh?" I gasped and turned in time to see Spencer roll over and slowly sit up.

A strangled scream stuck in my throat.

Spencer's blank eyes stared into mine.

"I'm dead," he whispered. "You're right, Diane. I'm really dead."

chapter

29

Cassie screamed and pressed her hands to her face. Lenny and Jordan backed up against the bare wall.

I couldn't move. I stood, stunned, and watched Spencer float up off the floor. He spun around in the air. Hovered about two feet off the floor. His long hair floated around his head like silver-white cobwebs.

He spread his arms wide and his mouth opened. An ugly black hole. He let out a ghoulish, bone-chilling laugh.

It's a joke! my mind screamed. A horrible trick.

But I couldn't see any wires holding him up.

Spencer floated closer to me. Cold air radiated off him. Moonlight streamed through the window, lighting up Spencer's decayed skin. His sunken eyes.

His evil grin.

Floating off the floor, Spencer stared down at me. "No more games, Diane," he rasped in his dry, dead voice. "No more Night Games. No games. I'm really dead. You killed me."

"Huh? What are you talking about?" I shrieked. "I didn't kill you."

"Yes, you did!" Spencer cried. He flew across the room and hung in a dim corner, pointing a bony, accusing finger at the four of us. "You all did! You killed me last year at the cabin."

"Spencer—" I started.

"All of you killed me," Spencer repeated. "You left me to die. You packed me under the snow and left me there. And I smothered in the snow."

His blank eyes returned to me. "You could have helped me, Diane. I thought you were my friend."

"I *was* your friend, Spencer!" I choked out.

"No, you weren't!" he screamed. "Friends don't let friends die, Diane. You could have stopped them. But you didn't."

He floated over me. An awful odor filled my nostrils. I coughed and covered my mouth.

What was he talking about? We didn't kill him. It had just been a stupid game. A snowball fight.

We didn't kill him.

Did we?

Suddenly I wasn't so sure. Did we do something terrible—and not realize it?

"If you're dead, how can you be here?" I demanded.

Spencer dropped to the floor. "My hatred kept me here," he rasped. "After I died, I climbed out of the snow. It took me a long time to realize what happened. But my hatred for you all kept me here in Shadyside."

He slid closer to me. "It kept me here long enough to pay you back. Long enough to scare you to death!"

I gasped. "You killed Mr. Crowell! You killed him! Didn't you?"

"I gave him a heart attack," he confessed. "It was part of my plan."

"What plan?" I whispered.

"I convinced you to come play the Night Games," Spencer explained. "I knew you couldn't resist. It was my turn to play a game on you—on all of you."

Spencer twirled around in the air.

He came to a sudden stop. "I had so much fun," he rasped. "Watching you all get more and more scared from my calls and notes."

"Why didn't you just kill us?" I cried.

"What kind of game is that?" Spencer demanded.

Then, without warning, he grabbed me.

"Now the game is over," he cried. "Now I'm going to kill you. The way you killed me."

I tried to pull away, but he was too strong. "You're my favorite, Diane," he said. "So you die first."

I screamed.

And then I couldn't make another sound.

His bony hands tightened around my throat.

I pushed at his hands. He squeezed tighter. Tighter.

I twisted and punched him with my fists.

He didn't seem to feel my punches. "Now this is fun. Really fun, Diane," he howled at me.

I clawed at his strong fingers, tried to pry them away.

NIGHT GAMES

A rushing sound filled my ears. I couldn't breathe.
No air. No air.
I felt as if my lungs were about to burst.
And then I didn't care anymore.
I sank into a comforting sea of black.

chapter
30

"No, Diane."

I heard my own voice. Scolding myself.

"No, Diane. You can't die now."

"Hold on, Diane. Hold on."

Out of the deep, deep blackness, an idea came to me.

With my last strength, I threw my arms around Spencer.

The creepy, rubbery feel of his decaying body made me shiver.

I hugged him hard.

I ignored the sour, putrid smell. I ignored the cold sponginess of his skin.

I hugged him harder.

His eyes widened in surprise. He loosened his grip around my throat. I swallowed air. Coughed. Struggled to breathe.

Spencer's dry, raspy voice filled the room. "What are you doing?" he demanded.

I forced myself to speak. "I'm hugging you," I told him. "I like you, Spencer. I've always liked you."

His fingers relaxed more. I took another deep breath.

"You said I was your favorite," I whispered. "I'm hugging you, Spencer."

His grip eased on my throat. Enough for me to turn my head. To signal to my friends.

Cassie moved quickly up to Spencer. She put her arms around him.

"What are you doing?" he shrieked, trying to push us off.

"We're hugging you, Spencer," I repeated. "We like you."

"No!" he screeched. "Get away from me! Get away! I need my hatred. I need my hatred to keep me here!"

I could barely breathe, but I kept hugging him. I forced myself to stroke his back. Touch his hair.

So disgusting. I wanted to retch. But I forced myself to hug him.

Lenny and Jordan joined Cassie and me. They put their arms around Spencer. They hugged him.

We all held on, hugging him. Hugging him.

"No!" Spencer wailed. "No! Let go of me! I need my hatred!"

I hugged him harder. "We missed you, Spencer," I whispered. "We missed you so much."

"You're our friend," Lenny whispered, hugging Spencer tightly.

"You're our friend, and we love you," I whispered. "We love you."

And as I whispered, I felt Spencer's shoulders soften. Felt his cold skin grow warm.

Warm and wet. Like melting snow.

I felt a shiver run through his body. I held on. Hugging him. Hugging him.

Feeling him soften and melt.

Yes. He was melting away. Melting like snow in the spring. Melting . . . melting.

"Good-bye, Spencer," I whispered.

And stepped back as his body melted to the floor.

We all stepped back. And gazed down at the wet, blue puddle on the dark floor. The puddle, glistening in the gray light from the window.

And then the puddle vanished, too.

The four of us stared down at the bare floor. And then raised our eyes joyfully to each other.

"He's gone," Cassie murmured.

"It's over!" Lenny cried.

Jordan let out a shout of happiness and relief.

Cassie and Lenny joined in. Jumping up and down. Shouting and crying and doing a wild dance of celebration.

I wanted to join in. But I felt so cold.

My teeth chattered. I hugged myself, trying to get warm, trying to draw another deep breath.

But I couldn't. Because I was dead.

In that instant—that cold, cold moment—I realized I was dead.

Spencer had killed me. Spencer had strangled me.

My friends celebrated happily—and I was dead.

It's not fair, I thought bitterly, watching them dance and hug each other. Why should they be alive while I am dead?

Lenny came over, flashing his wide grin. He hugged me, and I felt only cold.

Bitter cold.

A few minutes ago, he stood here and watched Spencer kill me. All three of them stood and watched me die.

They didn't move. They didn't help.

And now they wanted to celebrate.

I stared at Lenny. I let him hug me, but I didn't feel a thing.

Should I tell them? I wondered.

Should I tell them that I'm dead now?

Or should I wait—and play some games of my own?

About the Author

"Where do you get your ideas?"

That's the question that R. L. Stine is asked most often. "I don't know where my ideas come from," he says. "But I do know that I have a lot more scary stories in my mind that I can't wait to write."

So far, he has written over fifty mysteries and thrillers for young people, all of them bestsellers.

Bob grew up in Columbus, Ohio. Today he lives in an apartment near Central Park in New York City with his wife, Jane, and son, Matt.

THE NIGHTMARES
NEVER END . . .
WHEN YOU VISIT

Next . . .
SILENT NIGHT 3
(Coming mid-November 1996)

Rich, snobby Reva Dalby is back in Shadyside!

Reva is home from college for Christmas break, and she's bored. So she decides to take over the holiday fashion show at the store her daddy owns—Dalby's Department Store.

Reva has a great time telling all the models what to do. Until the models start dying one by one—strangled by the colorful scarves featured in Reva's show.

Reva isn't bored anymore. Now she's terrified. Will she be next on the killer's list?